Something In The Air...

"Look, we both know there was a little more going on here than just a friendly kiss," Sam said.

"Was there? I didn't notice," Maggie replied tartly.

Boy, was she ever something, Sam thought. Talk about blind stubborness! "In case it slipped your mind, Ms. Duncan, I just kissed the living daylights out of you. No—don't thank me. I'm a generous guy by nature, and you're about the neediest case I've run across in a long time. So now, how do I get out of this house?"

He shifted around so that his backside was facing her, and it was all the prompting Maggie required. Carefully planting one booted foot an inch from his behind, she stiffened her knee, shoving him out the flimsy door.

Dear Reader:

Happy New Year!

It takes two to tango, and we've declared 1989 as the "Year of the Man" at Silhouette Desire. We're honoring that perfect partner, the magnificent male, the one without whom there would *be* no romance. January marks the beginning of a twelve-month extravaganza spotlighting one book each month as a tribute to the Silhouette Desire hero—our *Man of the Month*!

Created by your favorite authors, you'll find these men are utterly irresistible. You'll be swept away by Diana Palmer's Mr. January (whom some might remember from a brief appearance in *Fit for a King*), and Joan Hohl's Mr. February is every woman's idea of the perfect Valentine....

Don't let these men get away!

Yours,

Isabel Swift
Senior Editor & Editorial Coordinator

DIXIE BROWNING
Thin Ice

Silhouette Desire
Published by Silhouette Books New York
America's Publisher of Contemporary Romance

SILHOUETTE BOOKS
300 East 42nd St., New York, N.Y. 10017

ISBN: 0-373-05474-2

First Silhouette Books printing January 1989

Printed in the U.S.A.

Books by Dixie Browning

Silhouette Romance

Unreasonable Summer #12
Tumbled Wall #38
Chance Tomorrow #53
Wren of Paradise #73
East of Today #93
Winter Blossom #113
Renegade Player #142
Island on the Hill #164
Logic of the Heart #172
Loving Rescue #191
A Secret Valentine #203
Practical Dreamer #221
Visible Heart #275
Journey to Quiet Waters #292
The Love Thing #305
First Things Last #323
Something for Herself #381
Reluctant Dreamer #460
A Matter of Timing #527

Silhouette Special Edition

Finders Keepers #50
Reach Out to Cherish #110
Just Deserts #181
Time and Tide #205
By Any Other Name #228
The Security Man #314
Belonging #414

Silhouette Desire

Shadow of Yesterday #68
Image of Love #91
The Hawk and the Honey #111
Late Rising Moon #121
Stormwatch #169
The Tender Barbarian #188
Matchmaker's Moon #212
A Bird in Hand #234
In the Palm of Her Hand #264
A Winter Woman #324
There Once Was a Lover #337
Fate Takes a Holiday #403
Along Came Jones #427
Thin Ice #474

DIXIE BROWNING,

one of Silhouette's most prolific and popular authors, has written over thirty books since *Unreasonable Summer*, a Silhouette Romance, came out in 1980. She has also published books for the Desire and Special Edition lines. She is a charter member of Romance Writers of America, and her Romance *Renegade Player* won the Golden Medallion in 1983. A charismatic lecturer, Dixie has toured extensively for Silhouette Books, participating in "How To Write A Romance" workshops all over the country.

Dixie's family has made its home along the North Carolina coast for many generations, and it is there that she finds a great deal of inspiration. Along with her writing awards, Dixie has been acclaimed as a watercolor painter and was the first president of the Watercolor Society of North Carolina. She is also currently president of Browning Artworks, Ltd., a gallery featuring fine regional crafts on Hatteras Island. Although Dixie enjoys her traveling, she is always happy to return to North Carolina, where she and her husband make their home.

One

Maggie downshifted and took the rutted road at a bone-rattling thirty miles an hour. She'd gotten over the shock of discovering the obscenity painted across her front door but her normal serenity still wasn't entirely restored.

She'd seen it early this morning. For the first few moments she'd been paralyzed, but then sheer outrage had sent her flying to the shed for enough paint to cover the door and the splattered frame.

Who'd ever heard of vandalism at Duncan's Neck? There weren't that many people who even knew it was there. Even for those who did, it would hardly be worth the bother of driving so far off the beaten track just to spray a little paint or toss a few rolls of tissue.

All the same, she'd stopped by the sheriff's office while she was in town and reported it.

"I can't spare a deputy right now, Maggie," he'd apologized. "Probably just a bunch of kids fooling around. I

doubt if they'll bother you again. Didn't, uh, sign their
artwork, did they?''

Maggie hadn't appreciated his sense of humor. ''I
should have checked for fingerprints myself.''

''How about tire tracks?''

''I forgot to look. They didn't leave the paint can,
though.''

''Mmmm. Well, I'll try to send a man out later on today, see if we can pick up anything, but to tell you the
truth, most of this kind of stuff looks pretty much like all
the rest.''

Maggie had studied the toes of her yellow shoes. ''I'm
afraid I went ahead and repainted the door before I left
home.'' Having cooled off somewhat, she was embarrassed at having stupidly destroyed the evidence before
she'd even reported the crime. ''I guess I should've
waited, but I was just so steamed I had to do *something*.''

''Unless there was a name, maybe initials—even the
name of a school—we probably wouldn't have been able
to tell much, but I doubt that it'll happen again, Maggie.
If it does, give us a call before you paint over it, and I'll
try to get a man out to look it over.''

''Tell your staff graphologist,'' she'd said sarcasti-
cally, ''that the writing was abominable and the spelling
was even worse. I'm still not sure if it was my house or my
hose that was insulted.''

To help rid herself of the awful feeling of having been
victimized, she'd driven directly from the sheriff's office
to her favorite shopping mall on the beach, where she had
indulged herself in a modest shopping spree and an expensive lunch. Now, feeling considerably better, she was
ready to unload her booty, change into her work clothes,

and put the final coat of paint on her six carved shore birds.

She drove right past the Peel cottage without even seeing the blue Range Rover, her mind focused on half a dozen more important matters. Who would look for a car where none should be?

Maggie's was the only insulated house on the wooded peninsula jutting out into the Alligator River. With insurance companies getting downright sticky about wood stoves and kerosene heaters, the seven other owners simply ceased renting their cottages out and closed down after Thanksgiving. But then, they were outsiders. Absentee landlords. Only Maggie belonged here.

She always celebrated after she'd seen the last of the renters off the property, knowing she would have the Neck all to herself until spring. Today, with the added excuse to pamper herself, she had browsed mindlessly for hours, finally treating herself to a jar of expensive moisturizer and a cassette tape she had coveted for ages. On the way back through Manteo, she'd stopped for groceries, steel wool, and a refill from the public library.

Forty-five minutes later she was back at her workbench, dressed in a flannel shirt and a pair of her grandfather's old bib overalls, humming along with Shostakovitch's Ninth as she brushed a wash of thinned waterbase paint over the shore birds she'd carved, then carefully patterned with a blowtorch. From a pan on top of the cast-iron range came the delectable aroma of a single chicken breast simmering in a rich, tarragon-seasoned broth of butter and Chablis. It was barely five o'clock, but already it was beginning to grow dark. A gust of wind rattled the windowpanes, making her think longingly of storm windows and spring.

As recently as a year ago, she would sometimes find herself pausing at odd moments and wondering how on earth she could have given up everything to hibernate in a place like Duncan's Neck. Doubts still crept in from time to time, especially when she was tired or discouraged. Like when one of the neighboring cottages had been left in a filthy mess, or when the plumbing jammed in one of the rentals that she oversaw and she had to unclog it while half a dozen burly sportsmen offered semi-helpful advice. Or times like today, when she'd stepped out onto her front porch and discovered that some ill-bred cretin had annointed her house with an unflattering, illiterate label.

So now the door of her gaunt, unpainted frame house sported a fresh coat of marine blue paint. Look on the bright side, Maggie told herself, rinsing her big oxhair brush and hanging it in its proper place—what if the only exterior paint she'd had on hand had been lilac? Or chartreuse? The door had needed painting, anyway. Come spring, she might even paint the window trim to match.

Sam Canady had caught a glimpse of the woman that morning and wondered who the devil she was and what she was doing intruding on his privacy. He'd had one hell of a time talking the rental agent into letting him have the place. The more reluctant the guy had been to give him the key, the more certain Sam had been that Duncan's Neck was precisely what he was looking for: isolated and uninhabited.

"They're just summer places, Mr....uh..."

"Canady," Sam had supplied. "Look, one of your regulars recommended this place to me. I'm not looking for luxury, just privacy." And then, at the suspicious narrowing of the agent's eyes, he had gone on to explain that his doctor had recommended rest and relaxation in a quiet place. Actually, it had been his secretary, Velma, not his doctor. And her recommendation had been rather more graphic.

"Well, you do understand that I'll have to have the whole month's rent in advance, plus the usual deposit for damage or loss."

"Naturally."

"We don't usually rent these places out of season. Now if you did want something in a beach cottage, I could—"

"No thanks. Duncan's Neck sounds just fine to me." He'd already checked out the beach strip. It was far from deserted, even at this time of year. If he'd wanted people around he could have found them without driving halfway across the state. He'd had any number of offers of female companionship since Laurel had died and he'd declined them all. Graciously, he hoped, but he wouldn't swear to it.

No, Sam's goals were simple enough; work his way through a few personal issues, cut down on his drinking and cut out smoking. Cold turkey. The last thing he needed was an audience, especially a female one!

By the time he'd driven on to Manteo, located the realtor's office, and then doubled back across the bridge, past Mann's Harbor and then some, it had been almost too dark to find the unmarked road. He'd found the right cottage—at least the key had fit—and it had been pretty much what he'd expected. Rough. Not to mention cold, damp, and uninviting. For the first few minutes, while he'd located something to cover the bare mattress and checked out the wood supply in futile hope of finding enough dry stuff to take the chill off the air, he'd almost regretted not taking the agent up on his offer of a beach cottage, complete with heat pump, hot tub, and electric blanket.

But then he'd reminded himself that he'd wanted to be alone, and this was about as alone as you could get. For business reasons, an ice floe somewhere in the North Atlantic was out of the question.

By the time he'd woken up the next morning, he'd been stiff from trying to keep warm under a ton of quilts, and his growling belly had reminded him that he hadn't bothered to unload the supplies before turning in. After dressing carefully so as not to accidentally chip off any frozen appendages, he'd headed out to the Rover to begin lugging in supplies.

That was when he'd seen her. She'd climbed into a mud-spattered red pickup and headed out toward the highway. He'd caught only a glimpse of long blue legs, yellow shoes, a yellow quilted jacket and a mop of long, shiny brown hair.

A meter reader for the power company, he'd told himself hopefully, but somehow, he couldn't quite make himself believe it. For one thing, no meter reader in his— or her—right mind would tackle this alluvial bog in yellow shoes.

He finished bringing in his supplies. None of the canned food seemed quite as appealing now as when he'd bought it. But then, food hadn't been one of his priorities in a long time.

Which was one of the reasons he was here, Sam reminded himself firmly. Too much work, too much booze, too many cigarettes, and too little of the things that were supposed to keep a man alive. Like food. Like sleep. Like peace of mind.

It had been two and a half years, almost three, since Laurel had been killed. Her clothes still hung in her closet. Her dressing table was just as she'd left it—cluttered with her makeup, smelling of her perfume. Every time he passed a woman wearing Giorgio, his gut tightened until he could scarcely breathe.

He'd moved into the den downstairs shortly after the accident, and now he seldom had reason to go upstairs at all. The maid who gave the place a going-over from time to time had offered to pack away Laurel's things and take them to her mother's. Sam had kept putting it off. Maybe after he went back . . . God knows it was past time.

The morning sun struck the river at an angle, dancing across the slight ripples on its surface. Today it was topaz; some days it was amethyst. On rare days it was black opal, dark and mysterious, with hints of color flickering just beneath the surface. Although Maggie's grandfather, Jubal Duncan, had explained refraction and reflection, and the way wind and sky affected the color of the water when she was ten, at thirty-four, she still preferred her own interpretation.

The broad, brackish river was only one of the things she loved about Duncan's Neck, which had been named after her great-great-something-or-other. Aside from the constantly changing beauty of the water, there was the dark, boggy forest and the narrow band of creamy-white sand that separated the two. She loved the cypress trees, feathery green in summer, bronze in autumn, starkly bare in winter, their roots writhing sinuously through sand and water like frozen serpents from a fantasy realm.

On the rare occasions when she thought about all she'd left behind, she reminded herself of all she'd gained in leaving it. No one can have it all. God knows, she'd learned that lesson. For a while, she'd honestly thought she could have everything—an exciting career, a handsome, successful husband, a lovely home in a fashionable area of Boston.

And a baby. Her baby. Her little girl.

"Stop it, Mary Margaret," she muttered grimly. She knew better than to look back, she really did. But now and then when she least expected it, the memories crept up on her, and she ached with the loss all over again.

Hard physical labor was an excellent remedy. She had split mountains of firewood that first year. She'd scraped the skiff, recalked every window in the house, and scrubbed until her knuckles bled.

Now, after four years, she'd learned to handle her emotions without going to such extremes. Cleaning seven cottages plus her own house, draining pipes, blacking wood stoves against rust, and lugging firewood or drift-wood for miles—those activities didn't leave a whole lot of energy for introspection.

On the other hand, it was peaceful here. No frantic rushing about, gobbling lunch with two phones ringing and a worried client on another line, no more trying to schedule time for her husband, her father, her mother, her clients, her co-workers, and still leave five minutes now and then for herself.

Freedom. That was what she had gained. Freedom from trying to follow in her father's footsteps, from trying to sound interested in her mother's social triumphs—freedom to damned well sit on a stump and count the leaves on a fig tree if she wanted to!

Which she seldom did. There was always walking when she felt restless. It never failed to put her in a wonderful frame of mind. Walking, she didn't have to analyze, she was free to simply enjoy.

Lacing on a pair of Jubal's lug-soled boots over two pairs of heavy woolen socks, she opened the door and tested the temperature. It was colder than it looked. She added a sweater and covered it with a canvas hunting coat that was older than she was, and then, sweeping her hair back, she jammed on the matching cap and tugged the brim down over her eyes. December or not, the sun was fierce today. She'd be a mass of squint lines soon enough without encouraging them.

In the two years since he'd died, Maggie had made good use of her grandfather's old hunting clothes. With an extra pair of heavy socks, even his boots fit well enough. Jubal had been a relatively small man, whereas Maggie was tall and long-boned but the clothes seemed to accommodate them both. Most of the things she'd worn in Boston would have been totally unsuitable for her present life-style. Her designer running togs and matching Reeboks were all very well, but she couldn't see herself making her usual round of supermarket, hardware store and library in a Brooks Brothers suit. She'd kept one or two basic outfits for unexpected occasions, which so far had failed to materialize, and had her secretary take the rest to the local thrift shop, including her brand-new maternity clothes and the infant things she'd begun to collect.

Especially those.

When she'd come running back to her father's old home, she hadn't really planned on spending the rest of her life there. She'd scarcely been capable of planning even one day ahead, and that was the way she had lived for the first year or so. One day at a time.

As it turned out, she'd never gone back to Boston. Her father, MacGuffie Duncan, financial guru and editor of *Duncan's Market Timer*, had visited several times, especially during those last few months before his father had died, and her mother usually spent a few days each fall in Kill Devil Hill, no more than an hour's drive away.

Her mother thought she was crazy for wasting herself in a place like Duncan's Neck.

"You'll come back when you're ready, girl," was her father's comment. "There's more than one kind of wealth, and more than one road to happiness."

Maggie was no longer interested in wealth, and at the moment, the road to happiness led along her favorite part of the beach, where she could stretch her legs, fill her lungs, and free her mind of any remaining dregs of the ugliness that had intruded on her world the day before.

Besides, there was a very practical reason to walk the shore this morning. She needed six perfect pieces of driftwood to use as mounts for the willets she had just finished. Not every piece would do, but she collected them all anyway. Sooner or later, she would find a use for them. Today she was looking for just the right size and shape to show off her carved shore birds without overpowering them.

And she was going to find precisely what she was looking for. She could feel it in her bones. Maggie had always been intuitive. Her father had claimed it was her intuition that had given her the edge over so many other brokers, that sixth sense of hers that knew exactly when a stock was going to take off. He wanted to believe it had been his teaching, plus her own training, but he'd finally admitted that she simply had the knack.

The knack, perhaps, but never the temperament, or even the desire. Only she couldn't have told him that without breaking his heart. He saw her as an extension of himself, just as her mother wanted to see her as today's version of yesterday's socialite.

But she was only Maggie, and she was beginning to think Maggie had been bent out of shape too long ever to grow into the person she was supposed to be.

"No introspection," she muttered, deliberately lengthening her stride. Soon she was whistling the theme of the symphony she had listened to the night before, hands in her pockets, cap pulled down to shield her eyes from the sun. "Hone it down to the basics, Maggie," old Jubal had been fond of saying. About decoy making, about food, about life in general.

She was proud to say that she'd finally honed her life down to the basics. Duncan's Neck was about as basic as it got. From time to time her mother sent her a care package—cosmetics, perfumes, canned truffles and pâté. Her father had given her a subscription to *The Wall Street Journal*, which she dumped in the trash unread. When it had expired, she had asked him not to renew it, as it was a total waste of her garbage space and his money.

"Aha!" Her eyes lit on a graceful arch of silvered wood half buried in the sand, and she swooped down and grabbed it. Unfortunately, the thing fought back. It was still attached to a tree some fifteen feet away.

With a shrug, she dusted the sand from her hands. So far she hadn't found a single piece of real driftwood, only cypress knees and boards that had washed ashore. She drew the line at sawing off the roots of a living tree, no matter how attractive they were, but if she didn't find something soon, she might consider bringing her chain saw and removing a few slices from some of the dead ones that loomed over the forest like ghostly sentinels. They were beautiful, and she hated to desecrate a single one, but her birds needed a perch, and she needed the money they would bring in once the shop reopened for the season and they were sold. Acting as caretaker wasn't quite enough to get by on, and she refused to touch her few remaining investments, having learned how transient security could be.

Admiring her own waffle-patterned tracks in the damp sand, she noticed for the first time another set of tracks. Frowning, she also noticed that they were going the same way she was. Had they come out of the woods? A trapper, or perhaps some nature-lover who had gotten himself lost?

Shading her eyes, she followed the footprints. They were large ones. Boot tracks. By the size of them, a man's. Those feet had been moving along at a fair clip, if she was any sort of tracker. Which she wasn't. Only an avid fan of nature programs.

And then she saw them. They appeared right under her nose, and she straightened up and nearly fell over backward.

The man reached out to steady her—or to push her away, she wasn't sure which. She had practically barreled into him. Against the sun, she couldn't tell a thing about him except that he was big and hard and carrying something that had stabbed her in the bosom.

Her first reaction was to demand that he leave, but then her wits began to return, and she remembered the vandal who had defaced her property. It was too much of a coincidence to be a coincidence—someone spray-painted her door, and a day later, she caught a stranger trespassing on her property.

"I beg your pardon," she said icily. A stupid comment, but she'd forgotten how to think under extreme pressure.

"You might look where you're going," the man responded, his voice about as soothing as a galvanized cut nail scraped along a fence. From what she could see, his looks weren't much better.

"You ran into me, not the other way around," she snapped. It occurred to her that his fingers were still

clamped onto her shoulders, and she twisted away and
stepped back. There was such a thing as personal space.
She didn't care to have hers violated by someone who
couldn't even spell four-letter words.

Maggie glared at him. For all she knew, he might be
glaring back. With his face in shadow, it was hard to tell.

She stepped to the side, and as she'd hoped he would,
he turned. Now that she could see him, she wasn't so sure
it had been a wise move. She should have walked away as
quickly as she could and shut herself in the house until she
was certain he was gone. For, although he was probably
the most striking man she'd ever seen, he was also one of
the most disconcerting. His hair was thick, curly and
completely gray. That was nothing in itself, but com-
bined with black, scowling brows and eyes narrowed to
the point where she couldn't even be sure of their color,
he was downright intimidating. In a lean, tanned face, his
nose was definitely on the aggressive side, and as for his
jaw, firm was an understatement. She had a sinking feeling that he'd be the very devil of a man to cross. Perhaps
she should try tact instead of threats. A little bit of dis-
cretion could disarm some of the most threatening animals...or so she'd heard on one of those nature programs.

It was then that her gaze strayed to his mouth. The
word that immediately sprung to Maggie's mind was sensuous, which was totally absurd. The man was glaring at
her as if *she* were trespassing on *his* territory. And there
was nothing at all sensuous about a mouth that turned
down at the corners—it simply indicated a nasty disposition.

Her own mouth had just opened to tender a tactful invitation to get the hell off her land before she called the
sheriff, when he leaned over and picked up the bundle
he'd apparently dropped when he'd barged into her. He

stepped back, all six-odd feet of him, and her mouth remained open as she saw what he was carrying.

Driftwood. *Her* driftwood! Tons of it, some still wet and sandy—at least a dozen pieces, no doubt including the very ones she needed to mount her six birds.

They continued to eye each other warily. Maggie stopped short—just barely—of demanding that he hand over the driftwood. "This stretch of shoreline isn't a part of the Alligator River National Wildlife Preserve, in case you happen to be lost," she said with what she considered admirable diplomacy.

"I was told that it belongs to a big lumber outfit."

He'd been told correctly. She tried a slightly different approach. "Some does, some doesn't. Technically, I suppose we're both trespassing, but since my family has been here as long as the Indians, I believe I'm entitled. Besides, I, uh, work as a sort of caretaker." For the cottages, not the lumber company, but she saw no need to embellish the simple truth.

He said nothing. Her eyes narrowed and her jaw began to jut. As much as she hated to admit it, the man was something to behold. She couldn't remember the last time she'd reacted to a man in such an instinctively... *physical* way. And that irritated her even more. Maggie was not accustomed to being affected by men. For the most part, she was indifferent. Even faced with a dubious character like this one, she had never allowed herself to be intimidated.

Nor was she intimidated now, dammit!

She watched for a sign of surrender and saw none. She still wasn't sure of their color, but his eyes were dark, with no hint of warmth. In fact, the hotter under the collar she got, the more glacial he appeared. If looks could speak, his could be loosely interpreted as, 'Stuff it, lady. I don't trust you and I'm not interested in whatever it is you're peddling.'

I'm not peddling anything! Except a one way ticket off my beach! "I see you're a driftwood collector," she said aloud, with more than a hint of challenge in her tone.

The man glanced down at the assortment of distorted shapes in his arms. "Firewood," he said shortly.

Firewood? Maggie felt her thin skin reacting to the force of her anger. That gorgeous chunk of curly-grained, red-and-silver cedar? He was going to *burn* it? Over her dead body.

It killed her to make the offer, but she had no choice. "I have some dry split oak that would burn a lot better," she said through clenched teeth. "If you're looking for color, try the beach. There's not enough phosphorus in the driftwood around here to make any sort of display in your fireplace."

"I don't have a fireplace."

"Well, if it's heat you want, you won't find that, either," she snapped. She was tempted to snatch it out of his arms and run, but from the look of his athletic build, she wouldn't get far.

Head tilted slightly, he studied her for a moment, as if wondering why she should care whether or not he froze to death. Actually, she didn't, but she reined in her temper and prepared to explain why she was willing to swap her valuable hardwood for his worthless scraps of soggy driftwood.

"No thanks," he said abruptly, and before she could argue, he pushed past her on the narrow beach and strode off toward the Neck.

Two

Sam dumped the wood on the back porch of his cottage and scattered it around with his foot so that it could begin to dry. Scowling at the suspicious haziness that was beginning to form over the west, he stomped the sand off his boots and let himself into the uninviting kitchen. When he got back, he was going to kill the so-called friend who had recommended this place as comfortable, but off the beaten track. It might be just dandy in August, but in December it was lousy! It sure as hell was well ventilated. In fact, it was colder inside than it was out.

And now this! He had deliberately steered clear of all the more civilized places because he'd needed to get off by himself for a few weeks. Now, dammit, it looked as if he wasn't even going to get that much of a break.

If he'd had to be stuck here with anyone, why not some old geezer who could disappear for days on end and turn up to play poker on the nights when Sam had trouble

sleeping? Or as long as he was wishing, why not wish for
an attractive, sophisticated woman who would appear in
his bed when he needed her and disappear when he didn't?
At least that would be useful. Sooner or later he was going
to have to get back into the swing of things. Man did not
live by work and racquetball alone.

His mind threw up an image of the woman on the
beach, and he swore fluently. She was going to be trouble. He'd had a funny feeling yesterday when he'd seen
her drive past. Yellow shoes and a red pickup, for heav-
en's sake! Now that he'd met her face-to-face, he knew for
sure that he was in for a hard time.

Sam was smart enough to recognize his vulnerabilities.
It didn't take an advanced degree in biology to know that
when a man hadn't been with a woman for almost three
years, certain pressures could build up. And those pressures could distort his judgment. And when those pressures were added to guilt and grief and God knows what
other little emotional time bombs that were ticking away
inside him, he owed it to the public in general and to
women in particular to stay the hell out of their way.

Which he was trying his best to do. The last thing he
needed was to be stuck out here in the back of beyond
with a woman! Or at least, not this type of woman. In
spite of the way she'd been dressed—the oversize boots,
the too-short jeans, and that canvas relic with all the sagging pockets—there'd been no mistaking the length and
the shapeliness of her legs. Not to mention the high
cheekbones, and the big, whiskey-colored eyes, and the
long, glossy brown hair that leaked out from under that
thing she'd been wearing on her head.

Uh-uh. She was bad news. He had a sneaking suspi-
cion that she was the sort of woman who stuck to a man
like flypaper once he was fool enough to get within range

of her. The rental agent had distinctly told him there was no one around but the caretaker. He'd figured some old guy would show up sooner or later to replenish his wood supply, and that would be it.

And then he'd seen the yellow shoes and the red pickup, and now he'd seen the hair and the eyes and the legs. And the mouth. Oh, God yes, that stubborn, opinionated, stark-naked mouth of hers that he hadn't been able to take his eyes off.

Oh, no. No way, Sam told himself with calm deliberation. He'd had all he wanted of women for the time being. His one and only close encounter had been disastrous. As a result he'd buried himself in his work for so long that now he didn't even know how to act around women anymore. He'd gotten an unlisted phone and spent little time at home. His secretary was old enough to be his mother, and smart enough to fend off the most determined female predator. His only other female contact was his dentist, and she was happily engaged. Besides, he could never get really turned on by a woman who smiled at him behind a mask while she carved away at his wisdom tooth.

Yet one look at that long-legged, whiskey-eyed creature swinging down the beach, and his body had automatically switched on circuits that hadn't been activated in years. It was downright scary!

With a grim expression, Sam reached into one of the cardboard boxes he'd hauled in before he'd hit the beach and brought out the bottle of bourbon. He regarded it steadily for several minutes. This had been his answer too many times when he'd worked himself into near exhaustion on a problem that defied solution. Unwind with a drink. Or two. Or three.

Well, he wasn't exhausted now. Frustrated, maybe...and cold. But alcohol was only a temporary solution, at best. And as damp and miserable as this dump was, he was in no real danger of hypothermia.

Hell, he was surrounded by trees. Some of the wood he'd picked up on the beach was probably dry enough to burn. The only problem was paper. He'd used all he could scrounge up, along with the few sticks of damp firewood he'd found on the porch, in an effort to start a fire in the kitchen stove that morning. He'd been hoping to heat enough water for instant coffee. The stuff hadn't even dissolved in the tepid water he'd produced, and he'd been in a foul mood ever since.

"Face it, Canady—it's the woman, not the cold. Or even the lack of coffee," he muttered, shoving the unopened bottle back into the carton. If he'd reached the stage where a tall, skinny scarecrow with a surly expression could get under his skin, he was in worse shape than he'd thought. All she had going for her was a pair of legs that wouldn't quit, a pair of interesting eyes and a decent set of cheekbones.

He sighed. Plus a mouth that looked full and soft and moist for the split second just before she'd set it in a thin line against him.

He swore and began slamming cans onto a shelf. Beans, spaghetti, soup—he hated canned soup! This whole thing was turning out to be an exercise in futility. He'd have done better to stick it out, fight his demons on their own turf, and then get on with his life.

The trouble was, there were too many reminders of Laurel back in Durham, he thought, idly tapping a can of salmon. His office, where they'd first met when he'd interviewed her for a job. He'd hired her, of course. She wasn't the sort of girl a man could easily turn away. Then there was the place where he'd taken her for dinner the night she'd told him she was pregnant. That had been two weeks later, and by then he'd been completely smitten.

"Did you check out our maternity policy before you applied for the job?" he'd asked. It was a generous one for a small firm—more generous than they could really afford.

"I—I didn't think about that," she'd whispered. "I only knew I was in trouble and alone, and I—Oh, Sam, what am I going to do? I'm so scared!"

Mesmerized, he'd watched her eyes brim with tears. She'd been good at tears. At the time, he hadn't known just how good. "Will you be wanting time off to get married?"

"He won't marry me. He can't, he...he's already married," she'd sobbed, breaking his heart. Sam had been ready to bawl with her by then.

"That bastard," he remembered muttering, and then, somehow she'd wound up in his arms, drenching his collar. He'd buried his face in her hair. The color of newly polished copper, it had smelled of Giorgio. His whole office had reeked of the stuff after she'd worked there a few days, but when it was on silky, red-gold curls, that was different. "What are you going to do? Will your parents help?" he'd managed to ask.

"I can't tell *them*! They'd disown me! Oh, Sam—" Up until a few minutes ago, he'd been Mr. Canady. "Sam, what am I going to do? I don't have anyone to turn to, and I—I do want my baby. One of my friends has a new baby, and it's so precious—it smells so sweet. But she has a husband and a nanny, and I don't have *anyone*."

It had all seemed so reasonable. He'd been thirty-five, with no commitments, no attachments. Home had been a furnished apartment. Convenient. Impersonal. Lonely.

"Look, Laurel, I know this is going to sound crazy, but hear me out before you say anything, okay?"

His apartment, of course, had been much too small, not to mention being in an unfashionable part of town. They'd bought the house soon after they were married, and Laurel had hired a decorator to do it over. She'd quit her job, of course, for it wasn't really suitable for Mrs. Samuel Adams Canady to work as a file clerk for SAC Environmental Consultants. Besides, she had a lot of socializing to do before she got too ungainly to be seen in public, she'd explained. Even a dried-up old workaholic like Sam should understand that. And of course, she'd wanted to show off their new home.

Actually, by that time, Sam was already missing his old apartment, not that he'd ever have admitted it aloud. Somehow, the picture he'd formed in his mind of marriage and fatherhood wasn't working out. Age might have been a factor. Laurel had been fifteen years his junior. It had been unrealistic to expect her to settle down the minute he slid a wedding ring on her finger.

Laurel's parents had been against the marriage from the start, not knowing the reasons for it. Still, they'd never been able to deny their only child anything, and if she wanted to marry a man almost old enough to be her father, so be it. As long as he could support her in proper fashion.

Within a couple months of their wedding, Sam had been trying desperately to convince himself that his bride was not really the immature, spoiled child she appeared to be. He put it down to hormones, to the emotional changes that went along with the physical ones.

Laurel had called him a stodgy old stuffed shirt— among other, less flattering things—a man who thought more about his stupid garbage dumps than he did about having fun.

He'd gone along with her idea of fun as far as he could. His eardrums had suffered, and so had his disposition. After working ten-hour days, he'd had little energy left over for traipsing from one party to another for the privilege of eating food he didn't like and having drinks shoved in his hands by kids half his age.

And so it had gone. Until the New Year's Eve when he had refused to take her to a party where one of her favorite groups was appearing live.

"It's beginning to drizzle. The streets will ice up before midnight," he'd told her. "Honey, in your condition, I don't think it's the thing to do, do you?"

"It's New Year's Eve! Naked Trash is going to be there! Besides, I see cars going by." Under the sheared beaver coat he'd given her for Christmas she'd been wearing a sequin-covered outfit that skimmed her full-breasted figure to end just above the knee.

"Laurel, be sensible. Conditions are getting worse by the minute—they've already issued a weather bulletin warning people to stay off the streets. We can walk next door to the Stevens's. They're having people over for drinks, and I sort of promised them—"

"Oh, wow! Let's hear it for the city councilwoman and her faithful consort, Fido. Geritol cocktails and cucumber sandwiches and a rousing discussion of the new sewage treatment plant! That's right up your alley, isn't it? And for all those under eighty, a little sweaty-palmed two-step dancing, right? Oh, you're hopeless, Samuel Canady. I should have known better than to let you talk me into this marriage in the first place!"

Sam had closed his eyes, his fist curling on the crumpled newspaper in his lap. He could have reminded her of a few things she'd forgotten, not the least being that she'd been the one to maneuver him into proposing. She'd admitted as much in one of their fights. On their honeymoon, she'd called his gray hair incredibly sexy, but the honeymoon hadn't lasted past the first bout of morning sickness. By the time New Year's Eve had rolled around, he hadn't really cared enough to argue.

He'd heard the front door slam, and tiredly—even reluctantly—he'd gone after her. He'd been too late. By the time he'd reached the street, the tail lights of the little convertible her parents had given her as a wedding gift were disappearing in the distance, leaving a wavering red trail behind on the wet pavement.

He could have moved faster. He damned well *should* have moved faster, but he'd been angry. So he'd stewed for a while, allowing his temper to cool. By the time he'd backed his own car cautiously out onto the street, conditions had worsened to the point where he'd had to creep along.

He'd finally located the place where the party was being given over in Chapel Hill, but he'd been too late. Laurel had been and gone. On learning that the rock group had been grounded at O'Hare, she had downed a glass of champagne and headed back to town to another party, accompanied by three of her friends. No—sorry, they didn't recall the address.

It had been almost two in the morning by the time he'd given up. With any luck, he figured she'd call him to come for her. By then it had been almost impossible to move without chains. It had taken him more than two hours just to get back home.

The police had met him there with the news. The wreck had been a bad one. The worst. No survivors.

For a week, he'd been numb. He'd let the Colliers, Laurel's parents, cry on his shoulder, lean on him, accuse him, and threaten him, and he'd taken it all in his stride. Laurel had been the center of their universe. She had been an increasingly small portion of his.

Which had brought on the guilt, and then the grief, and then more guilt. Sam had thrown himself into his work. After a while he'd been able to function almost normally. If he tended to skip meals and smoke too much—if the occasional drink before dinner had become the frequent drink instead of dinner—then it was no more than could be expected of a man under a lot of pressure. The environmental experts were being called on to solve quickly and cheaply all manner of problems man had been piling up since the beginning of the industrial revolution. It was a challenge, and God knows he'd needed a challenge just then. He'd needed anything to keep him from thinking of the vital young wife he'd lost and the unborn child she'd carried with her.

Tiredly, he stood up and stretched, his fingers brushing the narrow panels of the wooden ceiling. His shirttail slipped its moorings, and he reacted to the sudden draught on his back.

Wood. A fire. Dammit, he was going to have to get some heat in this dump sooner or later. He refused to eat another can of cold anything!

Striding out to the front porch, he glared across at the back of the unpainted house that stood between his place and the water. Smoke rose from the chimney and angled off across the river. The steady stream of fragrant wood smoke brought visions of a roaring fireplace and a gleaming kitchen range with all sorts of delectable smells issuing forth from an assortment of pots and pans.

A few hundred feet away, Maggie tipped her chair back and propped her socked feet on the chrome plated fender of the old black stove. With another sock, she buffed the waxed body of the wooden shorebird, pausing now and then to gaze at it with satisfaction. She'd call this one Deke, after her cousin in Manteo. She named all her creations, and this one had the same little beady black eyes as Deke.

In the utility room, the washing machine churned away with its load of linens. It was ridiculous to provide linens for cottages that had only the sketchiest of indoor plumbing. Still, once people got used to something, it was hard to change, and the same people had been renting the cottages on Duncan's Neck for years. It wasn't the sort of place to attract newcomers.

Stretching toward the table, she placed Deke alongside his mates. Six of them, all different, but all with that unmistakable attitude that made them instantly recognizable as a species. And all with that indefinable touch that made them recognizable as M. Duncan's work. She could hardly claim the prices Jubal had commanded for his decoys once they'd become collector's items, but give her time. She'd started whittling as a child during the summers she used to spend with her grandfather, but she'd really learned the art of wood carving when she'd moved back as an adult. She'd only been selling for three years now, but each year her work brought higher prices.

Maggie glanced out the window at the Peel place. She'd looked for signs of habitation when she'd gotten back from her walk and discovered the Rover. A.B., one of the realtors in Deke's office, should have let her know. It was his responsibility to keep the cottages rented in season, but it was hers to look after them. For all he knew, she could have already drained the pipes for the winter. Matter of fact, she had shut off the water heater.

She grinned. "Tough luck," she murmured to the row of birds in front of her. "Let him see how much water he can heat with that driftwood he stole from me. The creep!"

All the same, she swung her chair around so that she could just see one side of the Peel cottage. The side with a chimney. While she watched, a puff of smoke emerged and dissipated into the cold, clear air. She waited for another one, but it never came. She could have told him—in fact she *had* told him. There was no heat in damp driftwood. It was hardly her fault that the season's wood supply had been exhausted. It was up to A.B. to see that there was wood available for cooking and light heating in the fall, and if he wanted to squeeze out another commission, that was up to him. She wasn't obligated to provide firewood for the cottages; a man from East Lake did that.

Oh, all right, if Old Stoneface felt like chopping and splitting his own, she supposed she could lend him the tools. But first he'd have to ask. She'd offered to swap driftwood for her dry, split oak, and he'd refused. If he wanted to borrow her tools, he was going to have to do a bit of crawling.

Three

———

Maggie wrestled against the wind, finally getting the sheet pegged securely to the clothesline. It would be dry in no time at all, not a wrinkle in it, smelling of sunshine and fresh air. No dryer could compete with that, and certainly not at the price.

Bending over, she reached for a pillow slip. Yellow and white stripes for the Thurmond cottage, blue and white for the Peel place, solid white for the Kittrage's, and so on. The whole Neck had once been peopled with Duncans, but the younger ones had moved away, and the cottages had long since passed out of the family. Now the last remaining Duncan served as caretaker for the lot of them. Quite a comedown. Not that Maggie would have wanted the whole lot—she could barely pay the taxes on her own property. With all the resorts beginning to crop up along the river, tax values were skyrocketing.

She fought the wind for another sheet. With today's batch of laundry done, she would be free to tackle her latest project—a sea gull. She'd already cut out the plug with her band saw. Next came the creative part, the whittling and sanding and shaping that would turn a chunk of tupelo gum tree into one of those haughty, raucous, winddancers she so loved to watch. If she could only capture that proud lift of the head, the down-curved bill, the...

Oddly enough, instead of the gull, she had a mental picture of a man with wild hair blowing in the wind, mouth curled downward, his head tilted back at an arrogant angle. And she hoped to hell he was shivering in his boots! It was all she could do to supply her own firewood. Even with a chain saw, it was no easy job. Stoneface had no business being here. If he wanted wood, he could buy it himself. She refused to feel sorry for any idiot who had no better sense than to rent an unheated, uninsulated house in the dead of winter!

Sam stood at the front window, hearing the rattle of loose panes, feeling the wind leak through the cracks. He hadn't expected luxury, but this was ridiculous. The house had probably been well built some half a century ago. Since then, a makeshift bathroom and a jerry-built carport had been tacked on. The bathroom, like the rest of the house, was an open invitation to frostbite, but at least the plumbing worked. After a fashion. A twist of a corroded knob brought forth a horrendous rattling of pipes and a reluctant trickle of cold water. So far, he hadn't worked up the courage to shave.

While he watched, the woman appeared with a basket of laundry. As usual, she was dressed about as fashionably as your average landfill scavenger. He watched as she fought to keep a sheet from getting away from her, and his stomach growled.

Hunger, he concluded quickly. But from lack of food, or lack of women?

He glared at the backwoods Aphrodite wrestling with the laundry. What the devil was she trying to prove? They were six rutted, muddy miles from the highway, without a living soul in sight. Nobody needed that many linens.

Unless she had a flock of kids off at school somewhere, which meant she probably also had a husband. That was probably it. She was married to a fisherman, or maybe a guide. According to the guy who'd recommended it to him, this area was known for its fishing and hunting. Half the furred and finned population of the East Coast was available within easy shooting or casting distance. From the looks of the place so far, he wouldn't be surprised to see an eastern version of bigfoot come lurching out of these woods.

Morosely, Sam continued to watch as the washerwoman peeled away a wet sheet the wind had wrapped around her head. She flipped it expertly across the line and secured it with a handful of pegs, then stepped back to admire her handiwork. A gust of wind tore her faded canvas and corduroy cap from her head, sailing it across the clearing, and she put up a long, finely shaped hand to brush back the hair that swirled around her head like a flickering cloud of brown smoke.

Then she turned and bent over the basket, giving him a first-rate view of long, denim-clad legs and a neatly turned behind.

With a groan he wasn't even aware of having uttered, Sam wheeled away from the window and glared at the miserable potbellied stove. The thing sat smugly in the middle of a rusted pad, frustrating his every attempt at gaining its cooperation. When it came to roughing it, he was as good as the next guy—at least as long as he was provided with a decent propane camp stove or a charcoal grill. But this cast-iron relic had defeated him hands down. The damned thing didn't even obey the basic laws of physics!

A few hours later, Maggie was folding sheets in the kitchen when someone pounded on her back door. She'd just gotten off the phone with her cousin, Deke Elkins, so it wasn't him. Besides, he refused to drive his precious new BMW out to the Neck unless it was an absolute emergency.

Taking time to finish folding the sheet, she placed it carefully in the basket before crossing to open the door to what proved to be an unwelcome caller.

A cantankerous sea gull came strongly to mind as Maggie took in his jutting nose, glaring eyes, and that mouth of his that seemed permanently frozen into a scowl.

Maggie met his eyes in cool silence, making a courteous effort to hide her displeasure. She didn't like strangers poking around her property. She didn't like surprises of any sort, and she'd had more than enough of those just lately. Twice in the past week someone had called her up and grunted something unintelligible and vaguely threatening over the phone. And then there'd been that business with her door. She wasn't really frightened, but she'd had quite enough surprises.

"Yes?" she said without so much as a glimmer of hospitality.

"Are you supposed to be some sort of caretaker?"

"So?" She wasn't obligated to caretake people, only cottages. About twice each season she was called on to make that point quite clear, and she'd grown extremely adept at it.

Meeting his eyes, Maggie understood for the first time the principle behind laser surgery. In an effort to stare him down she felt her neck grow another inch. "Yes?" she repeated in her most regal tone.

"You mentioned some dry wood."

He sounded distinctly unimpressed. Evidently, she'd failed to quell him. She decided to try another tactic. "You've changed your mind about borrowing some of my firewood? What's the matter, couldn't you get a fire going with your lovely pieces of driftwood?"

"I would like to *buy* a few pieces of dry wood, just enough to last until I can make arrangements to have some delivered," he corrected stiffly. "Whatever you paid for it. Plus your trouble, of course."

The woman studied him as if he were some alien species, and Sam stood there, fighting the urge to tell her what she could do with her precious firewood. But the truth was, he needed her damned wood. What's more, he refused to be dismissed by some jerkwater female who looked as if she'd shatter if she ever tried to crack a smile.

Warm air flowed past her, laden with the scent of coffee, fresh laundry, and something essentially female. But it was the coffee that got to him. He sniffed involuntarily. He hadn't had a decent cup of coffee since he'd left home, and his gaze was drawn past the woman barring the doorway to the gray enameled pot on the gleaming black range behind her. Without meaning to, he sighed.

Later, Maggie would wonder what on earth had prompted her to invite him inside. She *hated* having strangers invade her territory. She valued her privacy far too much to open herself up to the sort of innuendo that inevitably came when a man realized she lived out here all

alone. Most of the regulars were a decent enough sort, if
a bit boisterous, but a few of them had let it be known that
hunting and fishing were not the only sports they enjoyed.

"Would you . . . like to come in for a moment?"

"Is that coffee I smell?"

Debatable, she thought, a spark of amusement appearing briefly in the amber depths of her eyes. She had
made it the old way, the way her grandfather had taught
her, boiling coffee grounds and water together and drib-
bling cold water down the side of the pan to settle it out.
Jubal had used egg shells. Maggie preferred the cold-
dribble method, even though it was not quite as effective. "Would you like a cup?" she asked, all innocence.

He didn't even need to reply. His frowning lips suddenly turned up at the corners, and she revised her esti-
mate of his age downward. Forty at the most. Possibly a
few years younger. Amazing what a change of expression
could do.

"Cream and sugar?" She waved him to one of the
scarred oak chairs at the kitchen table.

"Cream, please," he replied, and she noticed that his
voice was quite pleasant when he wasn't snarling. Deep,
quiet, firm.

She opened a can of evaporated milk and placed it on
the table along with the plain white cup, dime-store variety. Then, turning to the sink, she tilted the lid of the coffee pot and dribbled. She could feel his eyes watching her
every movement, and she barely restrained a smile. Maggie had a perfectly good Mr. Coffee machine in the pantry. Now and then she even used it, but as she seldom
drank more than one cup at a time, the old way was better. Drip coffee grew stale after an hour or so. Boiled coffee just grew more concentrated. By the time she got to the

bottom of the pot, she was usually diluting it half-and-half with milk.

She saw his gaze go to the box of wood shavings she used as tinder to build a fire. "Your husband's a carpenter?" he asked.

"No." She poured his coffee, and he eyed the red-and-white can warily.

"I'll just take it black. Uh, cholesterol, you know."

"Wise choice. Sorry it's not decaffeinated." She toned hers down several shades with milk and added three spoons of sugar.

Sam sipped, gasped, tried not to grimace, and set his cup down on a faded daisy in the freshly laundered tablecloth. "On the other hand, I skipped bacon and eggs this morning," he muttered, reaching for the can.

After that, there didn't seem to be much to say. He looked about him curiously, trying to discern just what made her hovel so different from his. Aside from the hot stove. And the coffee. And whatever it was that was sending out such a delectable aroma from the general vicinity of the range.

She had four straight chairs, a table, an elderly refrigerator, a rust-stained sink and a few cabinets. So did he. A few scraps of faded cloth here and there shouldn't make that much difference. Nor should the collection of blue bottles in the window, some of them not even clean. Or the old decoys scattered around the room. Her ceiling fixture was a bare bulb in the porcelain socket and so was his. There was a pair of men's boots, the canvas hunting coat and matching cap, plus a yellow slicker hanging beside the back door. His own coat was on a chair back in the kitchen. So much for the homey, lived-in look.

"Nice place you have here," he said, unsure even as he spoke whether he was being sincere or sarcastic.

"Thank you. I like it."

Not *we* like it, but *I* like it. Was that significant? And what the hell difference did it make if she did live here alone? he asked himself. She might be the local game warden. She could be the local bootlegger for all he cared, just as long as she kept out of his way.

He finished his coffee, wondering if the stuff could possibly be as caustic as it tasted. His gut was in bad enough shape without adding insult to injury. "I noticed some fallen trees a little way back in the woods. Would anyone mind if I helped myself?"

"Probably not," Maggie said equably.

"I, uh, wonder if you know where I might rent a saw and an ax. I didn't know I'd be needing them or I'd have brought along my own."

Meaning he knew how to use them, Maggie interpreted. She rather thought it had cost him something to make the request. "You're welcome to borrow mine. I use a maul and a wedge instead of an ax, though." Jubal's rusty ax was dull and it weighed a ton. She'd never been able to hit the same cut twice with it, much to his amusement.

"Thanks. I'll take good care of them, I assure you," he said gently.

Maggie shot him a veiled look as she sipped her cooling coffee. What had that particular tone of voice meant? It had been so long since she'd associated with the sort of people she felt obliged to read that she'd almost forgotten how. So much for instinct. Right now, hers was picking up a message that evidently had been garbled in transmission, because she knew damned well neither one of them was interested in what had just slipped through her mind.

All right, so he was a reasonably attractive man and she was a normal woman—even Jubal would have to agree that that was basic enough. But, basic or not, she wasn't interested. From the looks he was sending her at the moment, neither was he.

So where the dickens had that embarrassing idea sprung from, Maggie asked herself, feeling more threatened now than she had when she'd walked out onto her porch and discovered that abomination on her door.

"Tools?" Sam reminded her.

"Tools," she repeated blankly. And then, "Tools! Right! I'll get them for you—they're in the shed." Her first mistake had been in allowing him into her kitchen, of course. It had been so long since she'd been in the presence of such a potent dose of masculinity, she would have thought—if she'd thought about it at all—that she'd have been immune by now.

He stood, and Maggie wondered if he knew what she was thinking and was deliberately flaunting himself. "You needn't bother," he said with a slight thaw in his voice. "If you'll just tell me where I can find them, I'll be glad to get them."

"No problem," she said briskly, deciding it was time she took herself in hand. And then she almost tipped over her chair in her effort to remain cool and distant.

Sam's gaze followed her appreciatively, if somewhat reluctantly, from the untidy knot of glossy brown hair, to her arrow-straight back in the faded flannel shirt and the ancient bib overalls. They were about six inches too short. On her it looked good.

He moved up to help her with her coat just as she bent over to pick up her boots, and her backside bumped against his thigh. Instinctively, his hands went out to steady her, closing over her hips.

Both of them jumped away. She straightened up, giving him the freeze treatment, and he held out his hands at his sides, palms up. His palms were still sizzling, his pulse rate had doubled, and he wished desperately for a cigarette. His withdrawal symptoms were taking a bizarre turn. "Uh—sorry about that."

After one level look, Maggie bent again to the task of tying on her boots, careful to turn her back to the wall. Head down, face covered by the hair that had escaped its knot, she took her time fitting two pairs of wool socks into the boots and lacing them all the way up to the top instead of the halfway mark she usually settled for.

"You okay down there?"

"Mffpfffglumph," she muttered. Could there have been an ostrich in her family tree? There'd been a time when she'd been noted for her coolness under fire. Not even Black Monday had managed to catch her off guard. Evidently she'd left that trait behind, along with everything else.

Finally she snatched up her coat and jammed her arms in the sleeves, not giving him a chance to offer his help. Not that he seemed particularly inclined that way. "Well, come on," she snapped, shoving past him to get to the back door. "If you hope to get any wood cut today, you'd better get a move on."

Grim-faced, she slogged along in Jubal's boots, managing to stay two strides ahead. If he was beginning to get any funny ideas about her, it was time she set him straight. Although, now that she thought about it, she couldn't quite pinpoint anything specific. His grabbing her by the hips had been accidental—she'd bumped into him.

Which was getting to be a habit, she reminded herself—one she would have to break. The fact was, it wasn't so much what had happened but how it had affected her.

With anyone else, she would have laughed and begged his pardon, but for some reason, this man had rubbed her the wrong way the first time she'd ever seen him.

"What's that, a cistern?" he asked as they passed a rectangular concrete structure rising some three feet above the ground.

"*My* cistern," she stressed, marching toward the building set on pilings some distance from her back door. "Each house has its own. The groundwater's lousy. We use rain water, so conserve it if you don't mind."

Seeing as how he hadn't yet figured out how to get the water heater to work, Sam wasn't about to squander too much of the precious stuff on hot showers and the like. And, so far, cooking water had not been a problem. "About the hot-water heater..."

Oh, drat, she'd meant to turn it on again. "I turned off the pilot after the last people left. There wasn't supposed to be anyone else," she said just as they reached the shed. Her tone was openly accusing, and she glanced at him to see if he looked suitably chastened.

It was a mistake. In the harsh light of a clear winter day, his face was strangely compelling. Maggie did her best to avoid his eyes, her gaze lingering on the deep grooves on either side of his mouth, and the stubble on his forceful jaw. He hadn't shaved. His beard was darker than his hair, almost as dark as his brows...

Sam watched her eyes move over his face, touching on his mouth, his chin, his ears. He could feel it. He could almost feel her touching him. His muscles tensed, his fists clenched. His breath grew shallow, uneven. They were standing a good five feet apart. She was nothing to look at. Hell, neither was he, but unless he'd forgotten more than he thought these past few years, the tension between them wasn't entirely animosity.

God, those eyes of hers! They were incredible. He couldn't recall ever seeing hair and eyes that were both that rich, warm shade of honey brown. What a shame they were wasted on such an acidulous misfit.

"I guess I can relight it," Maggie said gruffly, turning away.

"Relight what?"

"Your pilot light, of course. Unless you don't plan to bathe or shave while you're here? Some men don't."

This whole thing had reached the point of being absurd, Sam decided. A look of amusement flickered in his eyes without disturbing the calm of his face. "I've considered it. Unfortunately, I never can get through the itchy stage of a beard, so hot water would be welcome."

"Fine," Maggie snapped.

"Great," Sam said, grinning broadly by now. Hell, he was on vacation. Just because he was stranded here with a witch, there was no reason for him to sink to her level. "By the way, my name's Sam Canady."

Maggie didn't want to know his name. She didn't want him here at all. For some reason—burnout, probably—he was getting on her nerves even more than the usual renters. It must be the season, she decided. Spring was hopeful, summer was cheerful, autumn was beautiful, but winter was simply bleak. Christmas was always a problem. Her mother refused to spend it at the Neck, her father refused to spend it without her mother, which left Maggie the choice of returning to Boston and all the memories or remaining here, alone.

"And yours?" Sam prompted, leaning up against a shed that was leaning in the other direction.

"My what?" Fumbling with the rusty hasp, she tried to pull herself back to the here and now. Living alone had its hazards.

"Your name. As long as we're going to be neighbors for the next few weeks, I may as well know what to call you."

Call me as rarely as possible, she was tempted to say, but that would have been childish. "Maggie Duncan," she said instead.

Sam's lips quirked up at the corners, causing her own to tighten in response. "Of the Duncan's Neck Duncans, I presume."

She shot him another quelling look and swung open the plank door, allowing light from outside to slant across the tar-papered floor. Legally she had been Maggie Leseur—Mary Margaret Duncan Leseur—until three years ago, when she'd petitioned the court to have her maiden name restored. "Help yourself," she said shortly. "Just be sure you put them back when you're finished. Things rust around here if they're left out overnight."

But Sam wasn't to be dismissed so quickly. "Hey, what the devil is this contraption?" Intrigued, he bent over and touched the chunk of rusty iron.

"That's my generator. The power's not too dependable, and once it goes off, it sometimes takes days for it to be restored. Here's the saw. There's an ax if you prefer, but it hasn't been sharpened in years."

Head bent under the low roof, Sam surveyed her tool shelf. The blade of a small chain saw was covered in what he recognized as a leg warmer. Laurel had worn them for a while, although she'd never gone in for either ballet or aerobics.

This one was pink. Sam tried to picture Maggie Duncan's long, slender legs encased in a pair of pink wool stovepipes, from her yellow shoes all the way up to...

Hastily, he turned and began collecting tools. "Well, look—I won't bother you any more. When I'm through,

I'll bring 'em back. Could I pay you for having your saw resharpened?''

"No need," Maggie said brusquely, anxious to see the last of him. "It's just been sharpened. Watch out for nails, barbed wire scraps and shotgun pellets, though."

The next two days passed peaceably enough. Maggie avoided Sam, who seemed equally intent on avoiding her. Her tools were returned, and the woodpile on the back stoop of the Peel cottage grew steadily. Smoke began to issue from the chimney, and Maggie stopped worrying about her unwelcome neighbor and concentrated on her sea gull.

She told herself that she could coexist with anyone for a month as long as they kept to themselves. And Sam did. If every time she looked at her pictures of gray-black gulls, with their surly attitudes and cranky expressions, she thought of him, that was hardly his fault. Maggie was essentially a fair person. She accepted responsibility for her own weaknesses. That, after all, had been the purpose of this whole exercise in self-reliance—to learn to live alone, dependent on no one. And not just to live alone, but to develop her own resources so that she actually enjoyed living alone.

And she did. For the most part.

Sam had been there five days when the Lone Ranger raided her garbage can. There was no mistaking his handiwork. Unlike her vandal, a raccoon was more interested in food. And the Lone Ranger was definitely a glutton. According to Jubal, raccoons were fastidious, often washing their food before they ate it. The Lone Ranger ate everything, sanitation be damned. He fought her for every fig on her tree, and she seldom got a chance at a persimmon. He ate them even before the frost hit them, which no one in his right mind would do.

She even left scraps out for him, hoping he'd spare her garbage. He polished those off first, and then tipped over the can to be sure she hadn't slipped up and thrown away an apple core or a crust of bread.

Not that Maggie was interested, but she couldn't help but notice that the shiny blue Rover remained parked under the dubious shelter of the Peel's carport. Canady was spending a great deal of his time in the woods. It wasn't that she watched, but when they were the only two people for miles around, she couldn't help but be *aware* of him.

He liked to walk. He had a wildly striped sweater she recognized as having cost a bundle, and he wore it to haul wood. Evidently he wasn't a clotheshorse. That, in Maggie's book, was a mark in his favor. Carlysle, her ex-husband, had spent far more time and money on his appearance than she ever had.

Sam had taken to walking the shore in the afternoons, so Maggie limited her walks to the morning hours. She waited until he had left before doing her outside work. Not that she was avoiding him. That would have been childish. All the same, there was no point in inviting trouble. Evidently he'd caught her at a bad time—a susceptible time. The thing was, she hadn't known she was susceptible until he'd come along.

Maggie was no babe in the woods. She'd been married; she'd led a perfectly normal life as far as sex was concerned, but she was no fanatic about it. In fact, if the truth were known, she was probably an underachiever when it came to that sort of thing. Putting as much energy into her career as she had—as they both had—neither she nor Carlysle had had much left over for the physical side of marriage.

At least, that's what she had told herself. At the time, she hadn't realized that Carlysle had been expending considerably more energy than she had in that respect.

"Oh, nuts," she muttered, paring wood furiously from the neck of her sea gull. As long as she didn't think about it, she didn't miss it. She'd gotten along just fine all these years, and now all of a sudden she was considering taking cold baths. In December yet!

The sound of her phone was a welcome interruption. If it turned out to be her prankster, she was in a mood to give as good as she got. She had a few threats of her own she could make if he didn't back off and leave her alone.

"Maggie, when are you coming to town?"

It was her cousin Deke. No greeting. Deke seldom wasted time on the amenities when it was only family. "I don't know. When I run out of everything, I suppose. Why?"

"I've got a proposition I want to put to you. How about driving over this evening? I'll treat you to dinner, okay?"

"Deke, I'm not in the mood to get cleaned up and—"

"Come as you are, then. We'll grab a double cheeseburger and fries at Hardees."

It was probably just what she needed, a good excuse to get away for an hour or two. She was getting stale. Besides, if she went early enough, she could exchange her library books. Deke was not one of her favorite people, even if he was her second cousin once removed. But family was family. Now and then, when she hadn't seen him for several weeks, she'd begin to think she might just be a tad unkind in her judgment of him, but then she'd run into him again, and they'd talk for a few minutes, and she would realize all over again that it wasn't her judgment that was off base. It was her cousin.

Deke was a hustler. Carlysle had been something of a hustler, too, if on a slightly different scale. Maggie had come to despise anything that resembled hustling. In some circles, wheeling and dealing was the norm, a polite way of pushing and shoving one's way to the top of the heap, but that didn't make it any more acceptable.

Carlysle had not been quite so ostentatious about his successes, but only because his background was the sort that frowned on vulgar display. In a way, Deke was almost endearingly naive, flashing his Rolex and his three-carat pinky diamond in a tiny, casual town like Manteo.

Maggie decided she'd been too hard on her cousin. "Okay, I'll come, but I want a shake, too. And this proposition of yours had better be worth the trip."

A few hours later, Deke laid out his proposal over the remains of their high-cholesterol feast. "How'd you like to find someone to take that old piece of termite bait off your hands?"

"What old piece of termite bait?" Maggie shook vinegar over her last french fry and nibbled it appreciatively.

Deke's laughter sounded slightly forced. "Come on, Mary Margaret, haven't you proved your point yet?"

"*My* point? I'm still trying to figure out *your* point." It must be something big, because she knew for a fact that now that he could afford the most expensive restaurants, Deke hated fast-food places almost as much as he hated being seen in public with her dressed in her work clothes.

It was obvious that he wanted something from her if he was offering to buy her house to sweeten her up. But what? She didn't have anything he could possibly want.

"I'm serious, Mary Margaret. I'm willing to pay you more than market value for that old dump because I worry about you living out there all alone. It's not safe."

"Oh, come on, Deke, we both know the place is nothing but a white elephant. The taxes have shot up and there's not a darned thing to show for it as far as I can tell. So tell me the truth, what do you really want from me? Stock tips? You'd be better off getting them from an astrologer. I'm out of it."

"You can't believe I'm concerned about you?"

"Nope," she said blithely, finishing off the last of her chocolate shake with more noise than was actually necessary just to see Deke cringe and look around to see who was watching.

"That side of the river is eroding so fast, one of these days you're going to open your door and step out into the river."

"Easy come, easy go," she quipped, stretching her legs out from under the table so that her muddy boots were in plain view.

"Have you seen all the new development they're doing along that stretch? Pretty fancy, huh? Windsurfing, sailing, waterskiing, and then, for the late fall season, a first-class hunting lodge with a walk-in fireplace and hot tubs on every level. You ought to drive up and look it over. Now I could picture you really enjoying a place like that. Same scenery as you've got now, but with all the comforts thrown in."

"No, thanks, I like my discomforts. I understand they're supposed to be good for building character."

"How did the tax revaluation hit you this year?"

"Right where it hurts, thanks to your Alligator Riviera. If you've got any clout with the other developers, tell 'em to stay away from my neck of the woods, will you?"

"You're against progress?"

"I'm all for progress as long as it doesn't come any closer to me."

Deke shot his cuff and angled his watch for the best light. Either he was showing off or she'd used up her allocation of his valuable time.

She toyed with the idea of ordering coffee. "So...what are you working on these days? Shopping malls? Condos? Squeezing a few thousand more bodies onto the beach?"

"How about a few million more dollars into the local economy?"

"You're too generous, Deke. Have you thought out a plan for when the whole beach is paved over and the tourists stop coming?"

"Why should they stop coming as long as we have the ocean? Mary Margaret, you're just being mule-headed. Did it ever occur to you that the people who come down here deserve a decent place to stay? And who do you think services the tourists? Who do you think depends on them for a livelihood?"

"Oh, so that's what you're up to!" Maggie couldn't help herself. She loved watching Deke's face grow red with frustration. He'd inherited the same thin skin she had. "You're going to build low-cost housing so that people can afford to work down here and service all these tourists you're bringing in?"

He sputtered something under his breath and dug out his billfold. It was ostrich, with gold initials. "That would hardly be cost effective. Look, if you're ready to go—"

"Sure. Thanks for the dinner, Deke—and thanks for the offer for my home, too, but I think I'll hang on to it. Who knows, I may rent out rooms to some of the locals who can't afford to live anywhere else."

"You're being facetious, but I'm really trying to do you a favor, Mary Margaret. As a matter of fact, I do have a selfish motive. Now I can't promise anything unless you make up your mind pretty fast, but there's this church group that's looking for a place to put a summer camp, and I could probably talk them into—"

"A summer camp? You've got to be kidding."

Deke ushered her outside, frowning at her muddy red pickup parked beside his immaculate BMW. Turning his back to the wind, he assumed a long-suffering tone. "Mary Margaret, be sensible. I'm trying to help you out because you're family, and family sticks together. You've had plenty of time to get over your divorce and come to your senses. Now, I've already talked to the other owners, and most of them are anxious to unload while there's still something there to sell. With the higher taxes, erosion, and all these new wetland restrictions I've heard are in the works, it won't be long before the place is completely worthless."

"Then why would any church group want it?"

He sighed heavily, his patience obviously strained to its limit. "Churches have special dispensation."

"On *wetlands*?" Not for a moment did she believe that. But then, not for a moment would she consider selling, so it didn't matter.

"Look, I've got a meeting—I'm already late," Deke said a little desperately.

"Don't let me keep you then." Maggie managed a genuine smile. He was a pest, and she didn't really like him very much, but he was family. "Thanks for worrying about me, Deke, but I'll be okay. I'll be just fine."

It was almost dark by the time she got home. The sky was layered with steely gray clouds that covered all but a streak or two of coral in the western sky. She parked in her usual place behind the house, gathered up her two sacks of groceries and the stack of library books, and picked her way over the rutted ground to the back stoop.

A form disengaged itself from the shadows and stepped forward.

"You had a visitor," Sam Canady said.

Startled, Maggie looked up. She felt the books begin to slide, and in an effort to balance them, lost her grip on one of the brown paper bags.

Four

Sam caught the egg carton in one hand and saved the sack with the other. "He said he'd be in touch later. Left his card."

Maggie had no choice but to invite him inside. In fact, it was Sam who opened the door she'd forgotten to lock, holding it for her to pass. "Put it on the table. Thanks for rescuing the eggs."

"Want 'em in the refrigerator?" Without waiting for her reply, he opened the door and looked for space. "Fish? Where'd you get fish? I've been wondering where around here I could find some tackle to rent, and maybe a guide."

He'd been wondering no such thing. It was the woman herself he'd been wondering about. He'd tried ignoring her and it hadn't worked. She stuck in his mind like a cocklebur, with her high cheekbones, her proud carriage and her long legs. Her voice was low, well modulated, her accent one he couldn't quite place. Definitely not local. All right, so he was curious. Who wouldn't be? A woman like Maggie, in a place like this?

Even as a small boy, Sam had never been able to resist a puzzle. It had been that same quirk in his nature that had led him into the field of chemical engineering in the first place, and from there to environmental problem-solving. He liked a challenge.

And Maggie Duncan was fast becoming a challenge.

He stashed the eggs and closed the refrigerator door in time to see her stretching on tiptoe to put a can of coffee on a top shelf. She must be about five foot nine or ten, he decided. The top of her head came about up to his eyes. Long legs, long torso, long hair. There was something about the woman that got to him, dammit. She was like an itch he couldn't quite reach to scratch.

"What? Oh, the fish." She folded the empty bag and shoved it into a basket. "They're mullet. I have a com-mercial fisherman friend who keeps me supplied. Those are corned."

Corned. Was he supposed to know what that meant? "Uh-huh," he muttered, reaching in the grocery sack for the last two items—a plastic bottle of cooking oil and one of shampoo. Honeysuckle scented shampoo. He'd have said she was more the tiger lily type.

"You don't have to do that. Please—I mean, thanks for helping me and for delivering the message, but I can manage by myself."

"No problem." He unscrewed the cap on the sham-poo, sniffed and then screwed it back on. "I've got noth-ing better to do."

"I'd really rather do it myself," Maggie said with em-phasis. Did she have to hit him over the head with a two-by-four to get the message across? She didn't need him, she didn't want him, she didn't like him!

"Plastic bottles, plastic bags, plastic gadgets—do you realize we're rapidly burying ourselves under a mountain range of non-biodegradable materials that are lethal to a large portion of the world's living creatures?"

A large baking potato in each hand, Maggie blinked twice and stared at him. "What? No—well, yes. Of course. Look, will you just—" Just what? Somehow, she couldn't quite bring herself to order him out of her house. "Thanks for your help, Mr. Canady. I can handle it from here."

Oh, he got the message, all right. She could tell just from the way his eyes narrowed. But instead of acting on it, he smiled at her, his teeth white and not quite perfect in his tanned face. Maggie felt her fingers tightening around her potatoes as she suppressed an urge to throw one at him. She decided that she liked him better when his lips turned down at the corners. Something about the man, especially that guileless smile of his, made her uneasy.

"Say, have you had dinner yet?" he asked suddenly. While they had been putting away her groceries, it had grown completely dark outside. The bare bulb overhead cast a yellowish glow over the center of the small kitchen, leaving the corners in shadow.

"Yes."

"Then how about dessert? I drove into Mann's Harbor today to see if I could find a heater, and while I was there I got some other stuff."

"A heater? What kind of a heater? I don't think the wiring will handle the load of an electric one, and as for the other kinds..."

"Don't worry, I'm not going to asphyxiate myself. The place is well ventilated, believe me."

"I was thinking more of your burning it down," Maggie said dryly.

"Ouch. Well, you're in luck. I decided that with two wood stoves, I should be able to stay warm enough. I'll go get the other stuff." He was out the door before she could tell him she wasn't interested in his "other stuff."

He made a quick dash from her house to his, almost hanging himself on her clothesline before he forced himself to slow down.

The fire had gone out again. The only heat he'd generated from his day's work with chain saw and maul had been body heat. Sweating like a Trojan, he'd cut, split, and hauled until the stoop looked like a fortress. So far, all he'd got for his labors was a fresh set of calluses and some sore muscles. The wood was either too green to burn or too far gone to generate more than a few lousy Btu's.

The sack was right there where he'd left it after he'd got back. Grabbing it, he paused before a clouded mirror on the kitchen wall, adjusting the collar that rode up above his heavy pullover. After raking his fingers through his hair a few times, he shrugged and gave up. The only time it had ever behaved was during boot camp right after he'd enlisted. It had been black then, the same as all the Canady men's. He'd been pretty proud of it—women seemed to like it a lot. But the Canady curls had been no match for a determined army barber.

Noticing the direction of his thoughts, he swore. What difference did it make what he looked like? Maggie was no great prize herself. When a beanstalk in bib overalls started looking good to him, it meant he was in even more trouble than he'd thought. He'd come here to be by himself and work a few kinks out of his system, not to impress the local talent.

"Hi, it's me—I'm back," he announced, closing the door behind him. "Say, do you always go off and leave your doors unlocked?"

Maggie pulled the door to her workroom shut behind her. He could stay in her kitchen for a few minutes—she'd allow him that much. But she would not have him poking his nose into her personal affairs. "There's no one to bother anything out here."

"You can't be sure of that."

She wasn't sure, at least not any more. She'd simply forgotten it today. Old habits were hard to break. "Anyway, there's nothing to bother," she said dismissively, running water into the gray pot.

Sam braced himself for another cup of her potent brew. He'd brought along one pint of Jim Beam and one pack of Salem regulars with the rest of his supplies. So far both seals were still intact. Even so, it was possible he could leave here in worse shape than he'd been in before.

Actually, the hardest habit to break was overworking. He hadn't considered that aspect of his self-imposed retreat. The woodcutting had helped, at least mentally. Physically, it had just about done him in.

"You may as well sit down." Maggie nodded to a chair as she put the canned milk and sugar bowl on the table. "Do we need plates for your, uh, stuff?"

Sam upended the sack over the table, spilling out an assortment of commercial sweets, including a package of cinnamon buns with the sugary icing chipping off the top and several brown and white items labeled Chocolate Flavored. "Depends on how fastidious you are, I guess. Napkins might be useful."

Maggie lifted her eyebrows at the heap of junk food on the table. "Talk about plastic," she said in an undertone. Sam's answering grin was vaguely apologetic.

They sat across from one another, poking at the assortment of sweets, studiously reading labels. Maggie grew increasingly aware of the man in her kitchen. A bit fancifully, she wondered if he were using more than his fair share of oxygen. Her own supply seemed strangely depleted. When he shifted in his chair so that his foot inadvertently bumped against hers, she actually gasped.

"The coffee ought to have boiled enough by now," she said breathlessly, jumping to her feet. It had barely begun to simmer.

"I forgot to give you this," Sam said, stretching to get into his pants pocket. He held out a business card, and Maggie reached for it cautiously. It still held the heat of his body. She felt her face growing warm.

The curse of having thin skin! She used gallons of moisturizer and pounds of night cream, and still it reacted to winter by turning all colors of the rainbow at the slightest provocation. "H. J. Wilkerson, Realtor. I don't know any H. J. Wilkerson."

"Seemed to think he knew you. At least, he mentioned a Duncan who owned a lot of property around here. That would be you?"

"Maybe. Maybe not." Somehow, Maggie found herself munching stale sugar buns and telling him about her great-great-something-or-other who had once made the finest moonshine on the east coast in a swamp not far from Duncan's Neck. "They called him Bearmeat. Don't ask me why. According to my grandfather, Jubal, Bearmeat Duncan owned practically everything in sight. Most of the land around here was considered pretty worthless—too wet to farm, too dry to fish. I don't think anyone else even wanted it, so he just sort of squatted and eventually got a deed for it. Jubal said his own father used to work for Bearmeat back in the twenties."

Sam polished off the last sticky bun and reached for one of the brown-and-white things. "I understand quite a few people were in the refreshment business in those days."

"Bearmeat didn't pick a particularly prominent location for his refreshment stand." Maggie accepted half of a brown-and-white thing and bit into it curiously. "Mmmm, grainy, but not bad. According to local rumor, his, uh—stand was so far up Tomcat Creek that the only way in was by boat. Every night he'd hang a lantern on one side and station a lookout on the other side. If the light blinked, that meant someone had passed between the lookout and the lantern and was headed up the creek in a boat. A runner was sent to warn Bearmeat."

"What happened then?" Sam added another dollop of canned milk to his coffee and sipped. He was developing a taste for it. As a foil for the sugary concoctions, it was downright tolerable.

Maggie shrugged, and Sam watched, fascinated, as the hollows above her collarbone deepened momentarily. "Who knows? I suppose it depended on whether they'd come to buy or to raid. Of course, Jubal would never admit to any first hand knowledge, but once when I was small, I overheard him reminiscing with an old friend, and I distinctly heard him say he used to serve as a runner for old Bearmeat. He might just have been bragging."

"Or he might have been trying to protect his innocent little granddaughter," Sam suggested.

"I seriously doubt that he was worried about my following in his footsteps. Although I'd have been proud to. Runner or not, he was the finest man I've ever known."

Sam said nothing. He was thinking about the various influences that could have produced a woman like Maggie Duncan.

While they'd been talking, the wind had risen until it shrieked around the corners of the house. Maggie got up once and used the poker on the fire.

"You've got that stove of yours tamed, haven't you?"

"I know its little quirks," she admitted modestly. Her face was glowing from the heat when she sat back down at the table, her eyes shadowed under the sweep of her long, straight lashes. She wore no makeup or jewelry. As far as Sam could tell, she'd made no attempt to fix herself up while he'd been gone. Evidently she figured he wasn't worth the trouble.

Dammit, at least he'd made an effort to tame his hair before he came back. Hers looked just as if she'd come in out of the wind. Any other woman would at least have smoothed out her collar. Not Maggie. It had rucked up on one side when she'd peeled off her coat, and she continued to ignore it.

Sam shifted restlessly in his oak chair, the unexpected détente that had sprung up between them somehow altered. The woman was beginning to irk him considerably. Worse still, he was beginning to look upon her as a challenge, and at this point in his life, the last thing he needed was another challenge.

"I hope coffee grounds are digestible," he said, biting down on one with a slight grimace. "Maggie, what are you doing in a place like this?" They'd gone through half his supply of junk food and finished off the pot of coffee. He wouldn't sleep for a week.

"It's my home." She lifted her chin in an unconscious gesture, and once more he found himself far too conscious of her body—her long, graceful throat, the hollows beneath those magnificent cheekbones of hers. He'd always admired tall women, even plain ones. Liked to watch them move. There was something inherently regal about a tall woman who carried herself well. And Maggie did. Nor could she ever be described as plain.

"Were you born here? Where's the rest of your family?"

"Is this the year of the census? Here, have another brown thing. I wonder what they make artificial chocolate flavoring from?"

"You don't really want to know. Does anyone else live out here year-round?"

"Not now. The white stuff isn't really cream filling, you know. It's C-R-E-M-E. When they misspell it, that's a dead giveaway. Do you eat a lot of this sort of thing?"

"At least it provides some body heat and doesn't require cooking," he said with growing exasperation. He'd dealt with some evasive characters in his work as an environmental consultant. He'd match her up against the slipperiest.

"Uh-oh. Still having trouble with your stove? You must not have gone far enough into the woods for your logs. I've already got the closest ones."

"If I'd gone any farther, I'd have needed a team of pack mules."

"I'm not sure pack mules work in teams. I think teams are the ones you harness together for plowing. How about an elephant? I've heard they're used for logging in some parts of the world." Maggie found herself enjoying their repartee. It was that enjoyment that made her push back her chair and begin gathering up the coffee things. No point in getting used to this sort of thing.

Sam took the hint. Somewhat to her surprise, he suddenly seemed as eager to leave as she was to see him go.

The wariness had returned full force on both sides by the time they stood beside her back door.

"I've got a lot to do tomorrow," she said. "The weatherman mentioned a front that'd be headed this way by tomorrow night."

"Oh, yeah—well, I'll be seeing you around. Thanks for the coffee."

"Thanks for the, uh, stuff."

For just an instant, something wonderful happened to his eyes. Maggie discovered that she couldn't look away. And then he smiled that slow, startlingly sweet smile, and she sighed and swallowed hard.

"G'night, Maggie Duncan," he said softly just before he leaned forward to brush his faintly chocolate-flavored lips against hers.

Then he was gone, leaving her standing there like a pillar of salt. After a moment, she licked her lips experimentally. Then, with a grunt of disgust, she slammed the door and thumbed the rusty night latch.

"This is plain dumb," she told herself firmly, as if the sound of her voice in the empty house would settle her turbulent feelings the way cold water settled coffee grounds. With brisk efficiency, she rinsed out the pot, banked the fire, and shook the crumbs from the tablecloth out the back door.

But against her will her gaze was drawn to the lighted kitchen window of the cottage across the clearing. Even as she watched, she saw the back door open. Sam stepped outside, his lean, broad-shouldered form clearly identifiable. He grabbed a few chunks of firewood and then disappeared inside again.

Maggie sighed. Then she selected a few pieces of split pine from her own supply, just enough to get the breakfast fire going, and hurried back inside. She spread the cloth back on the scarred wooden table, turned off the light, and hurried to the icy bathroom to get ready for bed. She had a brand-new historical by one of her favorite authors, and she could hardly wait to dip into it.

Tonight had been a mistake, she told herself, laying aside the unopened book some time later. She should have known better. She'd deliberately weaned herself away from dependence on everything, including people, when she'd left Boston. Having her grandfather here with her for the first two years had made the transition easier. Now she could go for days, even weeks if she cared to, without hearing the sound of another voice. She was truly self-sufficient. Having proved that to herself, she was not about to weaken and let herself start craving the company of other people. Of men. Of one man in particular.

The willets were done and the gull wasn't going well. For some reason, she found herself unable to concentrate. Maggie knew she needed to get away, but she was well stocked with groceries and library books, and she couldn't think of another reason to drive into Manteo, much less all the way out to the beach. She always ended up spending money she could ill afford when she went to town.

The most sensible thing to do would be to forget the gull and spend a few hours making sketches in her blind. Evidently she hadn't done her homework well enough before she'd cut her plug. Or maybe she should put the gull aside and try a belted kingfisher. She had some scraps of wood that would do well enough for smaller projects, and she was beginning to think she needed some variety in her life.

The blind was one Jubal had used for occasional hunting. It had been built on a framework atop a flat-bottomed boat that had washed ashore a couple of years ago and gradually filled with sand. Maggie had used it as a birdwatching station ever since.

Neither Jubal nor Maggie had done much hunting. Maggie liked roast duck as well as the next person, but she was constitutionally unable to kill the feathered creatures she spent so many hours watching. Now and then one of her grandfather's friends would come by with a Canada goose, all plucked and drawn. She never turned it down, even though it was too much for one person to finish off. The Lone Ranger usually got the leftovers.

Half an hour later, she'd made herself comfortable in the small brush enclosure near the edge of the water, sketch pad and drawing pencils ready to go. The only problem was that the birds seemed to have deserted her. There wasn't a duck or a goose to be seen, much less a gull. Not even a kingfisher. The familiar layers of clouds that had been hovering for days covered half the sky, but even so, the light on the water was fierce. By the time her feet were too numb to feel and her bottom damp from sitting on the sand floor, she hadn't made a single mark on her drawing pad.

So much for inspiration. Gathering her things, she took one last look through the interwoven brush walls. Something in the distance caught her eyes—a mere flicker of movement against the distant screen of trees, something about the size of a dog, with rusty-reddish coloring.

A dog? The closest ones were Junior Jones', about eight miles away, and they were blue ticks. Could it be—? Could it possibly be...?

Pressing her face between two prickly sticks, Maggie scrunched up her eyes against the silvery glare and scanned the area for another glimpse of the reddish-gray fur. Like everyone else in the area, she'd followed the progress of the rare red wolves that were being reintroduced into the natural environment in an experimental program, after being extinct in the wild for years. Several mated pairs that had been raised in captivity had been released in the Alligator River National Wildlife Refuge a few years previously, after undergoing a period of acclimatization. So far, the experiment seemed to be working well, but Maggie had never seen one of the elusive animals.

There! She saw it again—the quick movement, that distinctive coloration. It could have been a dog, but somehow, she was certain it was one of the red wolves.

Sam's voice caused her to jerk her face around with no regard to the scratchy brush wall. "Good morning," he called out cheerfully. "That is you inside that thing, isn't it, Maggie? Looks like those clouds really mean business this time, doesn't it?"

"Shhh!"

"Sorry—what did you say? The water's pretty noisy beating against the—"

"Hush! Just get *in* here, will you?" Maggie whispered fiercely. Dammit, why did he have to come along now? Or ever! If he hadn't already scared off her wolf, he soon would at the rate he was going. They were incredibly shy.

She heard him fumbling outside, and with an impatient grunt, she shoved open the door with her foot. Holding one finger over her lips in a plea for silence, she frowned while he folded his long limbs inside and pulled the door shut behind him.

"What's going on?" he murmured. "I didn't see any wildfowl."

"Of course not, with all the noise you're making! What are you doing out here? You're supposed to take your walk in the afternoons. The mornings are mine."

"They are? Is there some rule that says you actually have to own property here to be able to walk the beach before noon? You should have told me."

"There's no rule—at least, not an official one," she muttered, edging as far away as she could. The truth was, there was not enough room for both of them in what was essentially a one-man blind. Jubal had hunted alone, and he'd built his blind just large enough to contain one man, one shotgun, a can of sardines and a box of crackers. He had never told her what he drank as an accompaniment, but she had some ideas on the subject.

Grudgingly, Maggie shoved her sketch pad aside to make room for Sam's long legs. He picked it up. Seeing the blank page, he began to flip through it. "What's this?"

"Nothing," she said sullenly. Her red wolf—if it had been a red wolf—was long gone. The morning was wasted.

"Looks to me like a ball of yarn with legs."

"It's an action sketch," she defended. She'd never claimed to be an artist. She had books to show her the conformation and coloration—her sketches were meant only to show characteristic attitudes. Getting them down on paper impressed them in her mind so that she could transfer them to her finished carvings, thus bringing to life what otherwise would have been merely a stiff piece of wood in the shape of a bird. At least it was supposed to work that way. With the gull, she'd captured neither attitude nor conformation.

Jubal had taught her woodworking. She'd made decoys at first, crude working models from the plugs he'd roughed out with a saw. Since she didn't hunt, however, she'd soon turned her talents to other subjects, and in the four years she'd been living at the Neck, she'd developed her skill to the point where she'd found a ready market for all she could produce.

"Action sketch, hmm? The action being a ball of yarn in the process of unwinding?" Sam grinned, deepening the grooves in his cheeks and setting warm lights dancing in his eyes. They were so deeply set, she hadn't yet been able to tell their exact color. They seemed to be a mixture of brown and green and gray, dark and entirely too changeable to be trustworthy. Like the man himself.

"If you must know—" She broke off in exasperation. "Would you please get your bony knee out of my ribs? It's a sandpiper in a feeding position. Head down, tail up."

"Oh," he said with an exaggerated air of understanding.

"Forget it."

Sam laid the pad aside. She was so close he could smell the honeysuckle fragrance of her hair. As usual, it was in a wild tangle about her face. She'd evidently pinned it up earlier; a few strands were still anchored to one side of her head with a tortoise clip, the rest tumbling in a glossy brown waterfall over the shoulders of her faded denim coat.

What a mess she was, glaring at him as if she'd like to be able to snap her fingers and consign him to the farthest reaches of hell. He'd been determined to ignore her. God knows, he didn't need to cut himself a chunk of that sort of trouble, but she needed someone to wake her up, and he seemed to be the only one around.

What the hell, he thought as his gaze roamed over her stormy eyes and the belligerent set of her chin—he'd be gone in a few weeks. He could spare her that much time.

"You've scratched your cheek," he murmured, reaching out to touch the long red streak. "Tetanus up to date?"

Maggie jerked her head away from his hand. "I'm more concerned about rabies."

Giving her a mocking grin, he clicked his tongue. "And you were so hospitable last night. What's the matter, don't sweets agree with you?"

"*You* don't agree with me, Mr. Canady. I make it a policy never to fraternize with the transients. That includes you."

"The rise and fall of a beautiful friendship," he said with exaggerated pathos. "Last night we were Sam and Maggie. Today we're Mr. Canady and Maggie."

"Ms. Duncan," she corrected, and then, because the whole thing was becoming slightly farcical, her lips trembled against a smile. Coy posturing was hardly her style, but a woman had to have some defenses.

"You'll be glad to know I was able to cook breakfast for the first time, Ms. Duncan." Sam's eyes were laughing at her, even though his mouth had that slight downward tilt at the outer corners that had intrigued her against her will ever since the first time she'd laid eyes on him. "My coffee tasted flat, though."

"It's the rainwater. If you're not used to it..." Her voice trailed off as her gaze became enmeshed with his.

"Maybe you'll teach me how to make it your way," he suggested silkily, and she could have sworn he was referring to more than making coffee.

"Hmmmm?" She'd forgotten to breathe. There wasn't enough room to breathe! A tangling of limbs, a tilting of heads, and then his mouth was on hers, tentatively at first, but quickly revealing a hunger that seemed to feed on itself.

This time he did not taste of chocolate, but of his own masculine essence. At the first electrifying touch of his tongue, Maggie found her fingers curling into the thick knit of his sweater. There were too many layers between them, and no room to move. Her right leg was cramping, and she couldn't find her way under his sweater....

She tried to shift her leg without breaking contact with his mouth. She couldn't even remember the last time she'd been kissed—*really* kissed. She'd all but forgotten this wild, sweet compulsion that could spring up out of nowhere at the simple coming together of two sets of lips.

"Wait...no, let me—" Sam whispered against her chin.

"I've got to—my leg's about to—" She had found her way under his sweater and wrapped her arms around his waist, reveling in the rush of feelings that swept through her at the touch of his warm, hard strength.

Breathing heavily, Sam pressed her backward, following her down, until suddenly, her head and shoulders broke through the flimsy wall and she was dangling half inside and half outside the blind.

"God, I'm sorry, Maggie!" With a stricken look on his face, Sam attempted to pull her back inside, only to have the sleeve of his pullover catch on a sharp stick. When he rose to a crouching position in an effort to free it, his knee came down on her thigh.

"Get off me, you ox!"

"Oh, damn—!" He whipped the sweater off over his head, leaving it dangling. "Don't move—you've got a stick rammed up under your coat."

"Ouch! My hair's caught on something."

After several tries, both of them managed to get free. Maggie slung the hair out of her face with a blistering look at the man who was taking up three-quarters of the floor space in the wrecked duck blind.

Sam had unhooked his sweater, but made no attempt to put it back on despite the rapidly falling temperature. "Maggie, I'm sorry," he began, and would have said more but she cut him off.

"Don't talk to me. Don't touch me. Don't even look at me," she said fiercely.

"Hey, now wait a minute, lady, that wasn't all my doing, you know."

"All I know is that it would never have happened if you hadn't been there."

Sam regarded her steadily. He couldn't argue with that statement. He didn't try. "Look, we both know there was a little more going on here than your hair getting pulled and my sweater getting snagged."

"Was there? I didn't notice."

God, she was something. Talk about stubbornness! "In case it slipped your mind, *Ms*. Duncan, I just kissed the living daylights out of you. No—don't thank me. I'm a generous guy by nature, and you're about the neediest case I've run across in a long time. So now, how do I get out of here? I believe one of the walls still left standing is a door, right?"

He shifted around so that his backside was facing her, and that was all the prompting Maggie required. Carefully planting one booted foot an inch from his behind, she stiffened her knee, shoving him out the flimsy door.

He landed on two feet and one hand and quickly righted himself, turning to glare at her. "One of your bootlicking relatives—"

"That's boot*legging*!"

"—should've taught you some manners. All you had to do was ask me to leave."

Maggie closed her eyes and clenched everything clenchable—fists, teeth, and determination. "I'm asking. I'll personally refund every cent you paid in rent if you'll just get out of here and go somewhere else for the rest of your vacation."

Five

The rain came before dark, sweeping across the river like a gray silk curtain. Maggie barely had time to throw a tarpaulin over the wood on the porch and weight it down so that it wouldn't blow off. After spending the entire afternoon in her shop working on the sea gull, forcing herself to concentrate on the smooth, even-grained tupelo gum instead of what had happened earlier that morning, she was ready to pitch the whole damned thing into the fire. The more she worked on it, the more it was beginning to look like an adolescent chicken with an overgrown beak.

Sheer exasperation finally drove her into the kitchen in search of something to eat, preferably chocolate and preferably lots of it. Before turning on the light, she glanced out the window. The rain had slackened off to reveal a sickly yellow sunset, silhouetting the stark shape of the Peel cottage against a narrow band of pale sky. A single light shone from a window, but not a whiff of smoke rose from the chimney.

"Oh, for crying out loud," she exploded. Some people didn't have the sense to get in out of the rain! Or to get their firewood in out of it. So much for the fancy 4×4 Rover, the Banana Republic wardrobe and the macho sneer. Sam Canady was obviously a desk type whose idea of roughing it was drinking his beer from the can.

With more noise than was strictly necessary, Maggie took out an iron skillet and slammed it down on the stove. She might as well get started on the corned mullet. She'd mentioned once that she liked them, and now, every time he thought of it, her grandfather's old poker buddy brought her enough to feed a regiment. With the whole house reeking of the collards she'd put on earlier to cook, mullet wouldn't make much difference. The first meal she ever remembered eating in this house had been fried mullet, collard greens, and Jubal's thick, black coffee, served in battered aluminum dinnerware. The collard greens had been garnished with a generous dollop of hot-pepper vinegar, and accompanied by cornmeal dumplings the consistency and weight of wet concrete.

She'd cleaned her plate, and then stayed awake all night with a stomachache, but it had been worth it to see the look of pride on her grandfather's face. If her mother had been there, it would never have happened, but then her mother wouldn't be caught dead in Duncan's Neck. The year she had married his son, who had already been making a name for himself in financial circles, she had visited Jubal Duncan, perhaps picturing Duncan's Neck as being similar to Cove Neck on Long Island. After that she'd shuddered at the very mention of the place, but to her credit, she had not prevented MacGuffie Duncan from acquainting their only child with her rural heritage.

The grease began to smoke and Maggie grabbed a pot-holder and slid the skillet to the coolest part of the range top before reaching up to close the draft. Lately she couldn't seem to focus her mind on anything—which was a distinct disadvantage when one cooked with wood and worked with power tools. Her distraction was under-standable, considering that she had no sooner gotten over her end-of-season burnout when the annoying phone calls had started. And then the rolls of tissue that had fes-tooned every tree on the neck one morning, and the graf-fiti.

"And now this," she added irritably, plopping a fillet into the pan. Just when she thought she could handle anything that came along, *he* had to come along! Just when she thought she had come to terms with her ten-dency to think with her emotions and instinct rather than her intellect, she discovered that she was no more in con-trol than she'd ever been.

Her father used to tease her about such things as crying at parades and hiding under the covers with a flashlight to read romances when she was in junior high. Later on, he'd kidded her over picking stocks on a hunch, then backing up her choices with research, even though her hunches had almost always panned out.

But neither instinct nor intellect had saved her from making a disastrous mistake when it came to picking a husband.

And dammit, she told herself, stabbing a sizzling fillet with a fork, it didn't take much in the way of intellect to tell her that Sam Canady would be a mistake. She didn't know quite why, any more than she'd known why she could run her finger down a column and stop at a certain stock, and know that it would double within a year. There

was something about him that got under her skin, and the
sooner he left, the better off she'd be.

With her mind skittering back and forth from curly
gray hair and a down-tilted mouth to gray-feathered backs
and down-tilted beaks, she continued to work automatically until, looking down, she discovered that she'd peppered and cornmealed the whole pan of fillets, ready for
frying. Oh, for Pete's sake! She'd meant to cook two sides
and save the rest. Now she'd be eating fish cakes for a
week.

The fish cakes reminded her of Jubal, which always put
her in a better frame of mind. One of his favorite homi-
lies had been Waste Not, Want Not. He'd gone on to
prove it by getting more mileage out of a collard patch, a
pound net, and a fifty-pound sack of white beans than
any mortal she'd ever known. And while he'd never had
money to spare, he had managed to educate himself and
send three sons to college—no mean feat.

Thinking about Jubal took her mind off other matters, and she was humming under her breath, dodging hot
grease spatters as she fried up the strong-smelling fish,
when Sam knocked on her door. Not waiting for her to
open it, he poked his head inside, his damp, grinning face
banishing her warm feelings of nostalgia and contentment.

"Hi. Hate to bother you, but my wood seems to have
gotten wet," he said, just as if they'd parted on the best
of terms. "Could I borrow enough from you to heat a can
of soup for supper?"

If Maggie had thought she'd put the matter of Sam
Canady into perspective, she'd been kidding herself. One
look was all it took to send her hormones to their panic
stations.

With admirable restraint, she said, "Help yourself. Just fold back the tarp, but be sure to replace it when you're finished." She dropped another side of mullet into the sizzling fat.

"Feels good in here," Sam said from the open doorway. "Smells good, too."

She spared him a derisive look. Some cooking odors were enticing. Fried mullet and boiled collards were not among them.

When he continued to watch her as she deftly turned the crisp brown fillets, she began to fidget. For a woman of thirty-four who'd been married and divorced, a woman who'd been in line for a junior vice presidency before she was thirty, she had suddenly grown remarkably self-conscious. "Is your damper stuck?" she blurted out finally.

Sam blinked several times, looking as if he'd sleep-walked his way over and had just now woken up. "My damper? Oh. On the stove, you mean."

"Of course on the stove." She didn't actually add, "you idiot," but it was clearly implied. "If the stovepipe sags the least bit, or gets bumped out of line, the damper can jam. That's probably what's wrong with yours."

The damper. That twisty piece of wire that stuck out of the stovepipe. Now why the hell hadn't he remembered that? The last time he'd had any dealings with a wood stove he'd been about ten. They'd gone to a small ski lodge in Vermont for Christmas vacation. His father had spent his days on the slopes and his evenings in the more congenial atmosphere of the main lodge, while his mother, who had argued long and hard for Caneel Bay, had remained in their suite, assuaging her martyrdom with vodka martinis. Sam had guiltily stuck by her, feeding the fancy wood stove and reading dog-eared comics.

He'd learned to snorkel at Caneel the year before, and this year he'd really looked forward to learning to ski.

"Yeah, that's probably it—the damper. I'll put a little torque on it and see if I can pop it loose."

"Just don't pull the whole works down. The heating man comes out every year to clean out the chimneys and check everything over. If there's a problem, you can move into another cottage."

"I'll let you know." By now Sam was all the way into the kitchen, having closed the door behind him. Peering over her shoulder, he sniffed at the fish she was frying. "Smells good."

"Smells lousy. Tastes good," she corrected, trying to ignore the heat of his body on her back. Her face was flushed enough from the heat of the stove without this added inducement.

"Now I see where the corn comes in. That's cornmeal, right?"

She didn't want to get involved in this discussion. Or any discussion. With brisk efficiency, she took up another fillet, placing it with the rest on a brown paper bag, and then she dropped in the last piece and moved the skillet back to keep the grease from overheating. Fine-tuning the temperature on a wood stove was a tricky business.

"You did say they were corned?" Sam prompted, and Maggie shifted her elbow so that it connected with his middle. He was making her nervous, breathing down her neck that way.

"I said it was corned mullet, meaning it's been salted down," she said with exaggerated patience. "Haven't you ever heard of corned beef?"

"Sure. Oh. I see what you mean. Funny term, isn't it? Wonder where it came from?"

"How do I know?" she cried, waving her spatula wildly. "Look, do you want to eat or don't you? If you do, then get out two plates and put them up on the warming shelf!" The invitation had been based solely on intellectual considerations, Maggie assured herself. If she'd chased him out of her house with a broom, now *that* would have been an emotional response.

Sam hastened to obey. He'd been determined to keep out of her way after this morning's faux pas, but dammit, a man had to have firewood! Besides, she put his back up. If there was one thing that irritated him, it was a woman who went out of her way to prove that she could be as independent as a hog on ice.

Well, he'd show her. He hadn't come begging. He'd come over here with a simple request for a few sticks of wood, and she'd invited him to supper of her own free will. He'd be a fool to turn down an invitation to fish and collard greens and go home to another can of cold SpaghettiOs. He'd eat, take his wood, thank her politely and leave. After that, he'd make sure he stayed out of her way. She'd damned near killed him this morning, just because he'd misread her signals and thought she'd wanted him to kiss her.

Come to think of it, maybe he hadn't misread anything. Maybe she'd just got more than she'd bargained for and run scared. All he knew was that she'd turned to him with those big, soulful eyes, and her mouth had gone all soft and pouty, and they'd been cramped up in that crazy bush hut of hers...

With a sigh of sheer bafflement, Sam surveyed his loaded plate and then glanced up at the woman seated across the table from him, a layer of something that resembled sawdust dulling the sheen of her hair without in the least dulling the rare quality of her natural beauty. He

might not know which was the more tempting, but he sure
as hell knew which was the safer choice. He was an old
hand at indigestion. Broken bones and frostbite he could
do without.

"Man, I haven't had food like that in years," he said
some time later, tipping his chair back and gazing regret-
fully at his empty coffee cup.

Maggie was disappointed. She'd rather hoped he'd react
to her plain country fare the same way she'd reacted to her
grandfather's thick black coffee and hot-pepper vinegar
twenty-five years ago. But then, the night was young. It
took a while to settle. "I'm surprised you enjoyed it," she
said pleasantly enough. "Corned mullet is too strong for
some people, and not everyone likes collards."

"Ever had kippers? Not a lot of difference. As for the
greens, we had a cook once when I was a kid who swore
by them. Both my parents are doctors and neither one of
them is what you might call domestic. If it hadn't been for
Arvilla, we'd have starved."

Maggie tried and failed to look away from his slightly
crooked smile. She could feel herself being drawn closer
to the edge of an unseen crevasse. "I rather doubt it."

"Mother was from Connecticut. She and Arvilla went
about ten rounds a week on the issue of proper green
vegetables and how to cook them. I think it ended when
Arvilla seasoned fresh asparagus with salt pork and
stewed it all afternoon. Mother had brought home guests
for dinner that night."

Unexpectedly, Maggie chuckled. At the low, musical
sound, Sam looked almost startled. "Your mother and
mine sound a lot alike," she observed. "Mother's list of
socially acceptable vegetables does *not* include collards,
turnip greens, or *poke salet*."

"What about corned mullet?"

"It's not a vegetable."

"Fish are judged by a different standard?" He reached for the last fillet left on the platter and finished it off, wishing he dared risk another cup of the coal tar she called coffee. Wishing he had a cigarette.

"As far as Mother's concerned, mullet isn't even a fish, it's an abomination. Never mind being from Boston—as far as she's concerned, fish is salmon, sole, or mountain trout, broiled, poached, or sautéed in butter. Any fish that actually tastes like fish is taboo."

"Speaking of fish, I noticed a boat at the pier. Is it available to someone whose lineage includes half a dozen generations of city dwellers?"

"You're welcome to use it. There's an outboard motor in the shed, but it's just a three-horsepower job. I sold the big one."

"That lets out waterskiing, I guess."

Maggie had a fleeting image of a tanned and fit Sam Canady on water skis, his muscular thighs tensed against the pressure, his hard body gleaming wetly above and below a pair of skimpy—"There's, uh, some fishing gear in the shed," she said hastily. "You're welcome to use it if you want to. You can buy bait at that place by the bridge out on the highway."

"You wouldn't care to come along and show me the best places to fish, would you?"

She didn't have to think twice. Fishing? In a tiny boat, all alone together in such close quarters, miles from civilization? She'd definitely trust her instincts on this one. "No thanks, Sam. I'm going to be pretty busy for the next few days. The next few weeks, actually," she added hastily, in case he had any idea about postponing his trip for her convenience. Her gaze touched on the thick, unruly hair that made such a startling contrast to his tanned face, and she could actually feel herself drawing back into a protective shell. Even a turtle knew enough to retreat from danger.

Sam rose from the table slowly, as if to give her ample time to review his long, lean frame. He'd peeled off his sweater earlier—the same one he'd worn that morning—and now the breadth of his shoulders strained the seams of his blue chambray shirt. Carlysle had had a similar shirt, with all the pockets, flaps and tabs. On Carlysle it had looked absurd. On Sam it looked just right.

"Nice shirt," she said now.

"Thanks. My wife bought it for me."

Long into the night, Maggie heard the echo of those words. There'd been a hard edge in his voice when he'd spoken them. It was almost as if the words were stones, and he was using them to warn her off. As if she'd *needed* warning.

Heat simmered just under her skin at the memory of those few moments in his arms that morning—the feel of his lips on hers, his tongue taking possession of her mouth as if it had every right to it.

Forget it, she ordered herself. The trouble was, she'd never been good at taking orders, even her own. Before she could stop herself, she was recalling every detail of the way he'd looked—his strong hands with their long, square-tipped fingers, the creases fanning out from his eyes, the way the sun cast pale highlights on his rugged features. Even the masculine smell of him, and the sweet, minty taste of his mouth.

You're lusting after a married man, that's how desperate you are, Mary Margaret Duncan!

I am not lusting! Just because I admire a man's physique—just because I occasionally miss being held, being kissed, being—all those other things . . .

Maggie swore under her breath and punched her pillow down. Restlessly, she flopped over onto her stomach and tucked her fist against her mouth. She was divorced. That didn't mean she was dead from the neck down. What did other women do—have affairs? It wouldn't work for her. She would have to care for a man to go to bed with him, and if she cared for him, she would want more than a temporary affair. Which meant that when it was over, she would be right back where she was now. Lonely and needy.

Dammit, she refused to put herself in that position ever again. And that was not merely an intellectual decision, but an emotional one as well!

As if it had happened only last week, she could remember the way she'd felt the night she'd told Carlysle her big news. Coming on the heels of finding out that she was in line for the vice presidency, it had been almost too much. She'd been amazed and nervous and euphoric— almost as if she'd already been celebrating. The champagne was a special bottle they'd been saving until Carlysle was offered a partnership, but she'd felt the occasion warranted it.

"Carr, I got off early today so that I could stop by my gynecologist's," she said, pouring him a glass as soon as he'd taken off his topcoat and parked his briefcase. And then, because she couldn't hold it in another moment, she'd blurted it out. "Darling, guess what! We're pregnant!"

Carlysle had set his glass down untasted, his gray eyes narrowing on her. "I don't believe I heard you correctly, Maggie. Would you care to repeat that?"

Like a fool, she'd been too wrapped up in her own euphoria to realize that he was not receiving the news the same way she had. "Yes, you did, Carr—it's true. I don't have the flu, I'm not run down or overstressed—my blood pressure's slightly elevated, but nothing to worry about. I'm two months pregnant. That's why I've been so draggy lately."

He'd gone from disbelief to sarcasm, to icy, calm fury. "I thought I made it quite clear when we got married that children were not a part of my plans for the immediate future."

"Well, it's hardly the immediate future any longer, is it? I mean, we've been married for—"

"I won't have it."

She'd been feeling sick by then, sorry she'd drunk the half a glass of champagne. She'd just been so thrilled once she'd gotten over her initial shock, and so sure Carlysle would share her happiness. "But we've already got it," she'd whispered.

"Then get rid of it. We can't afford it."

"Good Lord, if we can't, who can? Besides, who are we going to leave it all to?"

Trying to reason with him had been a mistake. Hardly her first. The more they'd talked, the more emotional she had become, which gave Carlysle the advantage. He was a skilled lawyer, and she was no match for him at the best of times.

The argument had ended when she'd rushed to the bathroom, sick to her stomach. When she'd come out, he'd been gone. It wasn't the first night he'd stayed away. He kept a room near the office for nights when he would be working late. Not until after her divorce had she learned about his women. But by then, it had no longer mattered.

He'd been fair enough in the settlement, but the truth was, they'd lived up to the very limit of their double income. Except for a portfolio of high-grade municipals her father had given her when she'd graduated from Wharton, she'd been left with very little of her own. The luxury apartment had to go, of course. She'd traded her car for something more modest, and found herself a tiny apartment she could almost afford. Her vice presidency had been announced, and she'd accepted all the congratulations, genuine and otherwise, her mind more on daycare centers and pediatricians than moving into her new offices and breaking in an assistant.

It had been hectic. The market had been going through one of its roller-coaster periods, and she'd been on the phone from breakfast time to bedtime with frantic clients. Morning sickness had set in with a vengeance, and already she'd had to move the buttons on her waistbands and leave her suit jackets unbuttoned.

She'd bought pink for the baby. Yellow would have been safer, but all her instincts had told her it would be a girl. She'd even picked out a name. After a sickly couple of months, the market had rebounded, and she'd celebrated by buying herself an expensive maternity wardrobe, one she deemed suitable for the junior vice president of a large brokerage house.

And then she'd started spotting. At first her obstetrician had not been alarmed, but when it continued, and her blood pressure had not settled down, he had ordered complete bed rest until delivery.

There'd been no question of taking her work home with her. Her mother, who'd insisted she move back home until the baby was born, had forbade her father from even mentioning the market. Her reading material, her radio

and the small TV set in her room had been closely moni-
tored, all business programs strictly off-limits.

It had not been enough. She had lost her baby anyway
and nearly lost her will to live. Marian MacGuffie Duncan Leseur would have been starting school this year,
Maggie thought with an ache that went soul deep.

She hadn't cried in years. Not since she'd become a
practicing pragmatist, dealing with life on a strictly un-
emotional level. Poking an arm out from under the covers, she grabbed a handful of tissues from the bedside
table, wondering how on earth she had gone from thinking about Sam Canady to thinking about her baby
daughter.

Men, she remembered, blowing hard and mopping
tears. Thinking about Sam had reminded her of the
charming young attorney she had fallen in love with in her
first year out of college.

Well, at least Sam was no charmer. That was one thing
in his favor. Just the same, she'd better find plenty to keep
herself busy with until he got tired of playing pioneer and
went back to wherever it was he'd come from.

The garbage can was upset again. That damned masked
bandit was going to find a rattrap in there one of these
days! Enough was enough. She'd tried to be a cooperative neighbor, putting the choice stuff in a basin on the
ground where he could get it easily, but was that enough?
No, he had to spread her garbage all over the county!

If she stopped to clean it up first, she'd have to take
another bath before she left. If she waited, it would blow
all over the woods. With a grim expression, Maggie began collecting milk cans, bread wrappers, and used sand-
paper. She should have taken it to the Dumpster days ago,

but she hated to make the trip for one small can. It was thirteen miles, one way!

"The joys of country living," she muttered. When the last bit was collected and stowed in a new plastic bag, she marched over to her truck and tossed it into the back. Sam's words about the environmental impact of what she was doing came back to her, and she shrugged. One more plastic bag wasn't going to make much difference. Maybe she'd see about an incinerator while she was out. That way she could pollute the atmosphere instead of the earth.

Maggie kicked the mud off her yellow Reeboks and headed back inside to wash up. Yesterday's rain had turned the low terrain into a bog. As usual. It was her bog, and she loved it, but there were times when she really missed some of the trappings of civilization. Sidewalks, garbage collection...

A few minutes later, washed and lotioned, she hurried back outside. It was only then that she noticed the flat tire.

Make that tires. Plural.

"Well, damn," she uttered softly. Those were brand-new whitewalls. Practically. At least they were brand-new retreads only a few months old. For both of them to go flat at the same time could only mean they were defective. Struggling to hang on to her patience, she strode around to the other side of the truck where the jack and tire tool were kept, although she couldn't see what good one spare was going to do her when she had two flats.

Make that four flats.

She was still standing there, shoulders sagging, lips parted in dismay, when Sam strolled up. "Problem?" he asked.

"Problem? What makes you think I have a problem?" Was he blind as well as obnoxious? All she needed was to have some macho jerk come along and make stupid observations while she was trying to think what to do next. Fists curling in impotent anger, she cautioned herself against getting overwrought. Emotional outbursts never solved anything.

"I happen to have four flat tires, that's all. I should think that would be fairly obvious, even to you." And then she burst into tears.

Sam hated seeing a woman cry. Laurel had cried on the least provocation, but somehow, Maggie's tears were different. A bit gingerly, he took her in his arms, turning her away from the damage.

"I don't believe this," she protested, chin wobbling uncontrollably. "Four flat tires! And they're p-practically new!"

"Hey, look—it's okay," he murmured in his most soothing tones.

She wrenched herself away and glared at him. "Okay? If you think four flat tires is okay, you've got a warped sense of values!"

"Well, dammit, stop carrying on, and I'll see if I can figure out what's happened!" Some women cried softly. Maggie didn't. She was a noisy crier. Some women—notably his late wife—never even smeared their mascara when they cried. Maggie's eyes were red and so was the tip of her nose. She threw herself into crying, heart and soul, and for reasons he couldn't begin to fathom, Sam wanted nothing so much at that moment as to gather her to him and shelter her from flat tires, strewn garbage, and all the other ills of her world.

Instead, he walked slowly around the muddy red pickup, his frown growing deeper with each step. By the time he'd completed the circuit he'd come to the only possible conclusion. Someone had really done a job on Maggie's truck.

"One I could believe. Maybe even two." Her voice was almost under control by now. "But *four*? Either someone's playing another rotten trick on me, or that damned raccoon has learned to unscrew valve caps." She was trying to make it sound like a harmless prank because she couldn't afford to believe otherwise.

Sam wasn't buying it. She had an evasive look in her eyes, and her chin still had a tendency to crumple. "Maggie, have you ever had anything like this happen before?"

"You mean vandalism? Not unless you count tipped garbage cans and a bit of spray-paint."

His features took on an oddly flattened look. "Spray-paint?"

"You know how kids are—class of such-and-such. Beat such-and-such school. So-and-so loves what's-her-name."

"Then you pretty much know who did it?"

She watched a red-tailed hawk dive out of sight into the woods. "Not really. They didn't exactly mention any names, or a particular school."

He wasn't satisfied she was telling him everything she knew, not by a long shot. But if there was one thing he'd learned about Maggie Duncan it was that she was a stubborn woman. "Yeah, well...without a closer look I can't be sure, but I have a feeling somebody knifed your tires. So if you know anything you're not telling me, I'd suggest you tell the sheriff."

Six

It took a pot of coffee, plus a few more tears on Maggie's part and some very effective comforting on Sam's before they were ready to tackle the problem of four flats and one bald spare. Maggie gave up on trying to remain aloof. In spite of her denial, she was alarmed by this latest attack. A few phone calls, a few rolls of tissue, and a spray-painted obscenity had been infuriating, but hardly frightening.

Four tires attacked with a knife were a different matter.

Watching her, Sam admitted to himself that he'd been mildly interested—all right, downright intrigued—by the tall, beautiful termagant who tried so hard to cover her warmth and wit with a crust of ice. But seeing her shaken and vulnerable had plain knocked the socks off him. She'd taken one look at her ruined tires and that cool facade of hers had been shattered beyond redemption.

"Give me directions to the nearest dealer and I'll see what they can do about your tires." In the back of his mind was a half-formed idea of buying her a set of top-grade recaps and letting her think hers had been salvage-able. In spite of a few allusions to a different back-ground, she was obviously living pretty close to the edge.

"There's this place in Manteo..." Maggie said dully. "I'd better go with you."

It took some engineering, but with the help of two jacks and several concrete blocks, they managed to get all four tires off and into the back of the Rover, leaving his own spare behind. "What happens if you have a flat on the way in?" Maggie asked as they crossed the bridge over Croatan Sound.

"I feel lucky today."

"That's one of us," she said with a gloomy attempt at a smile, and Sam reached over and covered her hand with his, giving it a hard squeeze.

A few hours later, on the way home, she was still in an unnaturally quiet mood. Sam glanced at her out of the corner of his eye as he turned off US 64 onto the dirt road. Her arms were crossed over her chest, eyes staring straight ahead, bottom lip drooping in what he knew was not the invitation it appeared to be.

Dammit, that was *not* what she needed right now! She needed a friend, and he happened to be the only one around. Unfortunately, she'd insisted on standing in for the postmortem at the garage. There'd been no way to work out a deal with the attendant. All four tires had been a total loss, and he could tell from the way she'd handed over the check that it had just about wiped her out.

"Stop!" Maggie jerked forward against her shoulder harness as Sam slammed on his brakes, skidding several

yards in the muddy ruts. Four tires shifted in the back, slamming up against the two front seats.

"What's wrong? God, Maggie, you scared the—"

"There—just to the right of that big cedar."

He looked where she was pointing and saw nothing but trees and more trees. Second growth, third growth, scrub. "Okay, I'm looking. What now?"

"Oh, it's gone," she wailed softly. "Didn't you see *anything*?"

"Yeah, I saw some trees, a vine with some red berries on it, and either a hawk or a buzzard. I'm no expert on birds."

He was profoundly grateful to see some sign of emotion on her face, even it was only disappointment. She'd been a zombie the whole way home. Hell, he'd have tap-danced on the hood of his car if he'd thought it would make her smile.

Not for the first time, it occurred to Sam that he was getting in a little too deep, considering he'd known this woman less than two weeks. That had definitely not been on the agenda when he'd chosen to lower his stress load by holing up in Duncan's Neck until he broke a few destructive patterns.

What he wouldn't give for a smoke right now!

"It was a red wolf," Maggie said with quiet intensity. "I'm almost positive it was. Remember, I thought I saw one when we were in the blind?"

Sam lifted one bushy black eyebrow and had the satisfaction of seeing the color rise to her cheeks. He could still see the faint mark where she'd been scratched when he'd accidentally pushed her through the wall. "I remember what happened in the blind, all right, and it had nothing to do with any red wolf."

She snapped on the seat belt she'd unfastened when they'd stopped. "Oh, for goodness' sake, let's go home!"

Sam was happy to comply. If they'd stayed where they were much longer, he'd have been tempted to remind her of just what had happened when he'd held her in his arms and watched her frosty surface begin to thaw. He hadn't imagined that warm, sensuous woman who had worked her arms up under his sweater and stroked him feverishly while she returned his kisses. She could deny it until she turned blue in the face, but something had definitely flared up between them. He might be rusty, but no man could mistake a genuine response from a woman, however much she tried to deny it afterward.

However, this was no time to bring it up. "Wolf, huh? It's possible, I suppose. Something's sure been nosing around your garbage can."

"Oh, that's just the Lone Ranger, a sneaky, fat old raccoon. Wolves are much too shy to come anywhere near garbage cans."

Sam knew as much about wildlife as he did about Etruscan funeral rites. Less, in fact, for all that he was an environmentalist. All the same, he was relieved that she hadn't slipped back into her shell. Pulling into the clearing a few moments later, he switched off the engine and then glanced at her profile, noting the pure lines, the long, straight sweep of her lashes, the delicacy of her skin. There were blue shadows at her temples and with the angle of the sunlight coming through the windshield, he could see the beginning of two fine lines across her brow. He put her age at somewhere in the middle thirties and decided on the spot that it was a fascinating age for a woman.

Before he could reach across to open her door, Maggie let herself out and went around to the back. She began tugging on one of the tires, and Sam calmly removed her hand and placed it in the pocket of her yellow coat.

"When it comes to changing tires, I've got my own system, but thanks anyway. Tell you what—I'll swap you a tire job for a hot meal. I don't even care what it is. Surprise me."

Then, in a gesture more tender than he knew, he reached out to brush away a strand of hair that had blown across her face. His palm lingered on the cool velvet of her cheek, like steel on a magnet. Abruptly, he dropped his hand and turned away. "Yeah. Well—I'd better get on with it. Sun or no sun, I'm afraid we're in for more rain."

Inside the house, Maggie stepped out of her muddy sneakers and hung up her jacket. There was a streak of grime down the left front from one of the tires, and her hands were filthy. The service station's soapless, cold-water facilities had been less than effective.

Wandering into the bathroom, she stared at herself in the mirror, half-expecting to see the burning print of a large hand on her cheek where Sam had touched her. It still tingled, a simple physiological reaction, she told herself. Her face had been cold, his hand had been warm; a perfectly normal reaction.

As for the rubbery feeling in her knees, that was normal, too, after a morning like this one.

Cheese toast, she decided after washing up and brushing her hair. No, that really wasn't enough after all Sam had done for her. Hot dogs blackened in a skillet, with chili and onions? She didn't have any chili. Or any buns.

It would have to be fish cakes, then. While the potatoes boiled, she flaked the fillets she'd cooked the night before and minced the onion, humming under her breath. She'd always thought of humming as a sign of contentment, but perhaps it was more of a nervous mannerism.

Once the seasoned and floured patties were browning in the skillet, she chopped cabbage and made slaw, wishing she had some red peppers and fresh lime to add zest and color. Surveying the lot, she decided that while it wasn't fancy, it would have to do. One look out the window told her Sam would be finished in a few minutes, and if he was as hungry as she was, he'd care more about volume than aesthetics.

She caught herself humming again. Really, for a woman who had just blown her budget into the stratosphere, she was reacting awfully strangely. She'd bought those four new recaps in the middle of the summer with the interest payment on her municipals. The bonds would pay out again in January, but she'd been counting on that windfall to pay her property taxes and buy a couple of storm windows. So much for careful planning.

"Lady, if you want the whole male population of the Atlantic seaboard beating a path to your door, just let 'em get a drift of that aroma." Sam closed the door behind him and paused, his hair a mass of silvery windblown curls. Maggie knew a sudden craving to run her fingers through it.

"It's only fish cakes," she said gruffly. She fumbled in the drawer for silverware, dropped a fork on the floor, and swore under her breath.

"Whatever. I guess I'd better go over to my place and wash up first."

When he made no move to leave, Maggie nodded to a door. "Through there and turn right. Clean towels on the shelf. Help yourself."

While he was gone, she served the fish cakes and dished up the slaw. There were fig preserves and artichoke pickles put up by a woman from Wanchese, and she put those on and scanned the refrigerator for something exotic to round out the meal. Unfortunately, her budget no longer ran to exotic. Until the season reopened in May and her birds started selling again, she considered herself lucky that it ran to food at all.

Sam dried his face on the satin-monogrammed, peach-colored towel and inhaled deeply. Woman smells. Both in the kitchen and in the bathroom. He hadn't realized how much he'd missed them, eating out, living alone. There was a big bottle of something pink on the shelf beside her shampoo. Woman stuff. There was something incredibly intimate about a woman's personal toilet articles. Funny—he couldn't recall being so aware of it with Laurel.

Her soap smelled like honeysuckle, too, and he smiled. But then, replacing the towel on the rack, he noticed the monogram and the smile disappeared. L? Who was L?

With a shrug, he twitched the towel until it hung evenly, and then he stepped back, accidentally brushing against the long white terry cloth robe that hung from the back of the door. Before he could clamp a lid on it, his imagination was conjuring up a picture of a naked Maggie, her skin still flushed from her shower, stepping out of the tub and reaching for the voluminous garment as water streamed down her long legs and beaded on her small, high breasts.

"Down, boy," he muttered softly as his body reacted to the mental image. Bracing his shoulders against the cold, white-painted wall, he deliberately steered his thoughts into a safer channel. Like ruined tires and the kind of creeps who took pleasure in such destruction. He'd feel a hell of a lot better if the lowlife had stolen them. At least there was a motive, no matter how reprehensible, for theft. Vandalism was a wild card.

A few moments later, his libido under control, he let himself out of the small chilly bathroom. He passed through the living room with a keen, if cursory, glance that took in the white walls, several pieces of worn wicker furniture with colorful but faded cushions, a bookcase loaded well beyond its normal capacity, and two more doors, one of them open to reveal the corner of a white iron bed with a feather mattress that billowed like a giant souffle.

Unbidden, another mental image began taking shape, and he quickly slammed the door on it, stepping back into the inviting warmth of the kitchen.

"I have milk if you'd rather not have coffee," Maggie said.

"No, that's fine. I mean either one. Water will do."

"How about a beer? It's left over from summer—aged in aluminum."

"That'd be great. I worked up a thirst getting those tires on."

He could have kicked himself the minute the words slipped off his tongue. Amber eyes that had been glowing with a sort of half-shy expectancy a moment before clouded over as he watched. He could almost feel the frost forming again.

"I offered to help."

"I didn't need your help, Maggie. It's a one-man job."

"Well, at least you could let me repay you for your gas. You wasted a whole morning on my account."

Sam jerked his chair out angrily. "Dammit, Maggie, we settled all that! Now, are we eating or what? I didn't get breakfast this morning, and it's already afternoon."

It was later still when Sam left. The dark, ragged clouds had returned and the air was so thick with moisture that the distant shore had completely disappeared. Feeling an obscure need for physical activity, he borrowed the chain saw again and headed for the woods. A band of crows followed his progress, commenting freely when he blundered into one leaf-covered puddle after another. The first time he went into cold mud over his boots, he gave it up.

God, what a dismal dump! Why hadn't he headed for someplace civilized instead of going into exile? He could've been warm and dry right this very minute, sitting in a comfortable bar, listening to a jazz combo in the company of some attractive, uncomplicated woman.

The chorus of crows continued to mock his dour expression as he trudged back toward the clearing some half hour later, lugging the chain saw. There wasn't a tree worth cutting up within a five-mile range, as far as he could tell. They were all either eaten up with fungus, drowned in a bog, or still standing. And Maggie had taken pains to inform him that first day that gleaning the forest did not include cutting down standing timber.

His top-of-the-line hiking boots, caked with half a ton of mud, grew heavier with every step. Ice water had seeped through the supposedly waterproof seams until his feet felt like twin glaciers. Inside his deerskin gloves, his fingers were completely numb. In fact, the only thing warm about him was his temper, and that was damned near boiling!

Speaking of which, he'd forgotten to light the pilot under the water heater. So now he could look forward to a trickle of cold water in a rust-stained tub in an unheated bathroom.

"Hell," he muttered tiredly.

One thing was certain, he sure wasn't going begging for firewood again. Just being around that woman was hazardous to his health. She'd been downright chatty over lunch, telling him some tall tale about a man who'd been

installing a TV antenna on his chimney when a bear cub
had wandered into his yard. The fool had actually been
chasing the cub, going to make a pet of it, when Mama
Bear had showed up. He'd scrambled back up on the roof
and pulled the ladder after him, but by the time the female had finished expressing her displeasure, two rooms
of his house had been trashed, one window of his truck
had been broken, and his skiff had been bottomed and
sunk.

"The house I can understand," Maggie had com-
mented, "but I can't see a bear deliberately sinking a boat,
can you?"

"Huh?"

Unfortunately, the whole time she'd been talking, his
mind had been wandering. He'd been picturing that great
swollen feather bed he'd glimpsed through the door and
wondering what it would be like to remove her clothing,
piece by piece, and then lower her into its billowing
depths.

Uttering another fervent oath, he replaced the saw in
the shed and slammed the door behind him, disgusted
with his lack of mental control. He'd learned self-
discipline at an early age, and he'd always considered it
one of his better qualities. So what was happening to him?
He'd been able to put aside alcohol and cigarettes with
little or no trouble; why couldn't he do the same with
Maggie?

Here he was—wet, cold and tired, and all he could
think about was making love to a backwoods witch who
had all the sex appeal of a porcupine! If he had a grain of
sense, he'd be out of here in the time it took to throw his
gear into the Rover. Instead, he had a sinking feeling that
he was going to go on eating her food, bumming her fire-

wood, all the time trying to figure out how he could get her into his bed.

Or himself into hers. Hers was probably warmer.

Leaving his muddy boots on the back porch, Sam crossed the icy linoleum in damp socks, going straight to the row of cartons lining the kitchen cabinet. He rummaged around among the canned goods until his cold fingers closed over a small, rectangular package. Neatly ripping off half the foil top, he breathed in the deep, rich aroma of tobacco.

There were times when a man stood in desperate need of comfort. If he couldn't comfort himself with Maggie, he could at least indulge in his favorite vice. Where was the harm? He was a consenting adult; if he wanted to smoke, it was nobody's business but his own.

Clamping the cigarette between his teeth, he flipped open a half-filled book of paper matches and ruined the first one. And the second. And several more, until the floor was littered with their broken remains. He flung the cardboard case after them. It was damp. Like everything else in this damned forsaken mud-hole.

But wait—! Hadn't there been a box of wooden matches stored in a coffee can somewhere near the stove? He'd figured it was a guard against mice. Instead, it was probably a guard against the humidity.

He finally located it behind his shaving kit, only to discover that it was empty. His shoulders sagged, but his eyes took on a determined glint. The glove compartment. He distinctly remembered checking the glove compartment for flashlight, maps, tire gauge and spare fuses before he'd left Durham. He was almost sure he'd seen a book of matches.

Turning up his pants legs several notches, he stepped gingerly into his muddy boots and hurried around to the carport, where he'd parked the Rover after unloading Maggie's tires. It was one of the few relatively dry places around, shielded from the rain, yet open enough for the sun to reach.

He was leaning across the driver's seat, pawing through an assortment of junk, when he felt something nudge his ankle. Something cold and wet.

He froze. His first thought was of snakes—but they were supposed to be cold and *dry*, weren't they? Unless they happened to be water snakes. In which case, they might be cold and wet. And just about ankle high.

Sam was no more afraid of snakes than the next man— that is, if the next man happened to have a lifelong aversion to anything that crawled on its belly and smelled with its tongue. Cautiously, he peered down at his foot. Nothing. He began to ease one knee up onto the seat.

Then he felt it again. Only this time it was warm. Wet and warm.

Alligators? This was the Alligator River, all right, but he'd been led to understand that alligators seldom ventured so far north. Besides, they were reptiles, too. Of course, one of them could've adapted to the climate by adjusting his body thermostat upward.

This was stupid. He was a grown man, not a quivering jellyfish!

Drawing both feet into the cab, he slammed the door shut. Just to be on the safe side. Just until he figured out what was down there, he assured himself.

The Lone Ranger? Somehow, he didn't think so. All his instincts told him that this was something a little more alarming than a fat, garbage-can-raiding, persimmon-eating raccoon. Maybe one of Maggie's red wolves, he thought, picturing the great slavering jaws and neon eyes favored by the makers of horror films.

On the other hand, she'd said they were shy, hadn't she? Too shy to nose around a man's bare ankle? Maggie had said—

Black bears. The bear cub. "Judas priest," Sam intoned reverently. He had a baby bear sniffing around him, and any minute now Mama Bear was going to come barreling out of those woods and rock his Rover into kingdom come.

What with the clouds, it was almost too dark to make out much detail. He could see the faint shapes of the other cottages lined up around the shore, and to the west he could make out a few of the tallest cypresses silhouetted against the sky, but that was all. There could be a regiment of bears marching in formation and he wouldn't be able to see them.

The flashlight. As soon as he thought of it, he dismissed it. It was pretty powerful, but not powerful enough to reach the edge of the woods and pick out a mountain of black fur against a black forest. Besides, he didn't want to do anything that might give his position away. He wasn't sure if bears steered by sight or smell, but he wasn't in the mood to take chances.

He wished to hell he'd had time to take a bath.

Hard on the heels of that thought came another one. Thank God Maggie couldn't see him now. He could do without her heckling. She probably took such occurrences in stride, but while Sam had never considered himself a coward, where large animals with long claws and nasty tempers were concerned, he leaned toward the conservative side.

"Okay, Canady, as I see it you've got two choices."

Who was he kidding? He hadn't a clue. All the same, the sound of a human voice did something for his morale. Come to think of it, he did have two choices, neither of them particularly appealing. He could make a break for it and hope Mama Bear wasn't under there with her brat, or he could hole up inside the Rover until she got curious enough to remove a door and investigate.

And since bearproof doors had not been an available option when he'd bought his 4x4 last month, that pretty well narrowed it down.

"Okay, mates, here we go," he said, arming himself with the flashlight, the jack handle, and his most intrepid expression.

Cautiously, he opened the door.

"Yip! Yip-yip-yip!"

Yip? The sound had come from somewhere near the rear axle. Sam had braced himself against a possible *grrrr*. The high-pitched yapping sound threw him off stride. Ignoring his state of imminent peril for the moment, he leaned over and whistled softly.

"Here, baby, baby. C'mon out, little yipper, let's get a look at you before mama comes gunning for us both?" Okay, so he had a soft spot for small, helpless creatures.

He heard the growl then, plus a whimper, a whine, and a few more yips. Uh-oh. Tactical error. It was distinctly possible that he had Mama Bear, Papa Bear, and all three baby bears camping out under his vehicle. Let them figure out the logistics of fitting a ton or so of bear meat under something the size and height of the Rover—all he wanted to do was put in a fast call to the local wildlife office. One of the first things he'd had to learn when he'd gone into business for himself was the art of delegating. This was definitely a case in point.

"Okay, okay, I'm going," he murmured. "I'm leaving, see? You and your cubs are perfectly safe. I'm an animal lover from way back, honest. I can't even set a mousetrap."

He took another step back, keeping a wary eye on the patch of pale, dry grass that was barely visible around the Rover. He'd gone no more than five steps when something small and furry raced out, attacking his trailing bootlace, and tried to drag him under the car.

"What the hell—!" Sam jerked his foot away, and the thing came after him again. It wanted to play.

A *puppy*? "You're a dog!" he accused, letting it chew on the flapping tongue of his boot while the cold sweat that had formed on his body slowly began to dry. "Hell, you're nothing but a fat, feisty, noisy little mutt," he said, grinning broadly.

They were wild, but Sam had little trouble rounding them up. They were at the curious age. The bitch was another matter. She was cautious—not exactly unfriendly, but taking no chances. It took the better part of an hour to lure her inside the house, and even then, it was more the fact that he'd finally managed to load her babies into a cardboard carton and take them into the kitchen than the canned ravioli he trailed out from the carport to the back door that did it.

The poor old lady was half-starved, and nursing that hyperactive crew couldn't have been easy on her. Still, once she'd spotted her babies tumbling around in a big caron lined with the quilt off Sam's bed, she'd lost interest in the ravioli and stepped gingerly in with them, bathing his scent off before she'd allow them to nurse.

Sam didn't try to push it. He watched from the other side of the kitchen table. He'd placed the box behind the stove, which was cold at the moment, but it would be a good place later on, once he got a fire going.

He watched them for some forty-five minutes, not even aware until his face grew stiff that he was grinning from ear to ear. All right, so it was crazy. He didn't know the first thing about dogs, but he could learn, couldn't he? Hitching his chair closer, he braced his arms across his thighs and leaned over the box, conscious of a feeling of warmth and contentment.

"Hey, lady, what are you doing out here in the boonies?" he crooned, looking for some clue that would pinpoint a certain breed and finding none. They showed signs of being feral, but they weren't truly wild. The pups were small and fat, but without knowing whether the sire had been a Saint Bernard or a miniature poodle, it was hard to judge their age. The bitch was in far worse shape physically. She cringed whenever he lifted his hand, as if she'd been abused. There were still marks around her neck, indicating that she'd been tied and either had been released or had broken away.

At the thought of someone's having mistreated such a creature, Sam felt a stirring of deep-seated anger. He lifted one of the musky-smelling bundles of fur and held it cradled in his two hands. "Hey, boy, uh, girl. What were you doing in my carport, huh? Going to hitch a ride out of here? Can't say as I blame you, honey. It's wet and cold and lonesome, isn't it?" He nuzzled the pup, but at the bitch's anxious whines, he lowered it back into the box, where it immediately attached itself to one of her swollen dugs.

Cautiously, he reached out a hand and allowed the female to sniff it. Only when she touched his fingers with her tongue did he venture to pet her, and then he was almost sorry he had. Her head felt as if it had been peppered with buckshot. Ticks, fleas, plus an accumulation of Lord knows what else. You name it, she probably had it. He was beginning to itch a bit himself, come to think of it.

Sam put off going over to Maggie's as long as he could. If he showed up at mealtime, she might feel obligated to feed him again, and he didn't want that. No thanks. He would deal with his reawakened libido once he'd left this place behind. Until then, he'd do better to steer clear of feather beds, duck blinds and cozy dinners for two.

The trouble was, she was beginning to get to him on more than a purely physical level. That could only spell trouble. When and if he ever decided to get involved with a woman again, it would be with someone close to his own age, someone with a similar background, a woman who shared his interests. And preferably someone easy to get along with.

Maggie missed by a mile on every count. Except possibly age. They were within a compatible range there, but nothing else matched. He liked a woman to be soft and feminine . . . sort of womanly.

Still, he needed the name of a vet. He'd never had a dog of his own, since his mother had been allergic and there'd been no room for one in his life since then. As a scientist, he knew enough about chemical pesticides to know that de-fleaing a nursing litter would be tricky business. He'd leave the whole lot with the vet and tackle the cottage while they were gone, in case they'd left any mementos.

"Maggie, it's me—Sam! You in here?"

No answer. He followed the sound of music to the room that opened off the kitchen. He'd assumed it was a pantry. "Hey, Maggie," he began just as the whine of a power tool cut into the strains of something classical and vaguely familiar.

Sam's mouth fell open. He stood in the doorway and watched while she steered the chunk of wood in a curving pattern through the band saw. Not until it parted and she flicked the switch, stilling the high-pitched sound, did she look up and see him.

"Don't sneak up on me like that! I could've cut off an arm!"

"I didn't exactly sneak," Sam said defensively.

"No, you just materialized in my doorway like some great hulking spook!"

They were both practically yelling to be heard over the strident clash of cymbals and trumpets coming from a pair of speakers mounted over her workbench. Sam pointed at them. "Do we have to have that?"

"I like it! It's my favorite part!"

Maggie knew she was being unreasonable. True, he had scared her out of her wits by showing up that way, but to be fair, she wouldn't have heard him if he'd pounded the door down. For some reason she felt as if she needed to defend herself against him. "Sorry. But you really did startle me." She leaned across a belt sander and turned a knob, lowering the volume.

"I'm sorry, too. I guess there's no easy way to announce your presence under circumstances like these. Is all this, ah, yours?" He gestured around the well-equipped woodworking shop, his eyes never leaving her willowy, sawdust-covered figure.

"It is now. Wait'll I blow the dust off and we'll take a coffee break. I'm tired of standing, anyway." She switched on a small air compressor, playing the hose over her body while Sam watched in stunned amusement. How many more parts were there to the puzzle of Maggie Duncan?

In the kitchen she poured two cups of thick, muddy coffee, added hot milk from a pan on the back of the stove and handed him a cup, smiling at his skeptical look. "Go on, take it—you know you love my coffee."

"This is coffee? I thought maybe you were running core samples from the river bottom." He grinned, sipped, and grimaced, reaching for the pan of milk. "What do you do with all that stuff? I mean, how did you learn to use it? What I really mean is, what the devil is a woman like you doing in a place like this, using tools that even I don't know how to use?"

She had to smile. "Is it an ego thing with you, or are you just naturally a male chauvinist?"

"I'm serious, Maggie," said Sam, his reason for being there pushed out of his mind for the time being. "It's enough to find someone like you in a place like this, without—"

"I don't know what you mean by someone like me, but I think it's pretty obvious how you feel about this place."

"Come off it," he shot back. "You no more belong in a hole in the swamp like this than I do. So what are you doing here? Are you hiding out? And what's with all the power tools? If you're the local carpenter, then I'd have to say you're getting a little behind in your work. Most of the cottages look as if they'll go down in the next hard wind."

Maggie was torn between amusement and irritation. Where did he get off casting aspersions on Duncan's Neck? Just because it was isolated—just because it happened to be slightly muddy at the moment. Just because the houses were all old and unpainted, and a few things didn't work the way they were supposed to, and a few other things were rusty, and still other things sort of blew away...

"I like it. It suits me just fine. As a matter of fact, I intend to spend the rest of my life here," she declared with no more than half a dozen mental reservations. "As for the workshop, it belonged to my grandfather. He built boats when he was younger, and made decoys when he was older. Beautiful decoys. People collect them even now."

Sam's gaze went to the birds lined up on a half shelf and on top of one of the cabinets. He recognized the Canada goose and a mallard—the rest he couldn't identify as to species. There was a curving section of driftwood on which several smaller birds were arranged in varying poses. It was good. In fact, it was damned fine work. He could easily see why people would want to collect it.

"Jubal held a degree in forestry," Maggie continued. "He worked for a large lumber outfit until he retired at age sixty-eight. By then he'd put all his sons through college. I used to love to spend vacations with him, much to my mother's disgust."

"I knew you weren't a local product," Sam said triumphantly.

"Local enough. I wasn't born here, but half my roots are here."

"What about the other half?"

"Boston. Very proper and very stuffy. Sometimes I wonder how Daddy ever got mixed up with them. He's sort of got a foot in both camps."

A thought occurred to Sam, and he asked, "Who's L?"

Maggie frowned. "*Elle?* As in the French pronoun?"

"L as in the satin monogram on your towels."

Her eyes shifted from his, and he could have sworn she was going to evade the question, but she surprised him. "Leseur is my ex-husband's name. I had mine changed back after we were divorced."

Sam sipped his coffee in silence. So she was from Boston, from a very proper, very stuffy family. And she was divorced. The picture *still* didn't satisfy him. He told himself that he didn't want to get too involved with Maggie Duncan, and he even half believed it. "What did you do in Boston?"

"I worked for a brokerage house."

"What happened?" It was like a sore tooth. He had to keep probing, even though he knew it was a mistake.

"I believe the popular term is burnout." It would do, at any rate. She had no intention of telling him why she'd thrown away a six-figure income and buried herself down here. "Sam, did you want something in particular, or is this just a social call? I really do have a lot of work to do."

Seven

Maggie was still waiting for Sam's reply when the phone rang. Without taking her eyes from him, she reached for it, resenting the interruption. "Yes?" she murmured absently.

And then she froze. Sam, watching her closely, saw the color drain from her face, saw her eyes widen and her knuckles grow white as she clenched her hand around the phone. "Maggie, what is it?" he demanded softly.

"I want you to stop this," Maggie said with a desperate sort of quietness. "I've talked to the sheriff, and he—well, he knows who you are. If you ever set foot on my property again, or—or call me on the phone, he'll throw you in jail and I'll see that you don't get out again for the next fifty years."

"Maggie, for God's sake!" Sam lunged across the table and reached for the phone, but he was too late. She slammed it down hard enough to shatter the eardrum of whoever was on the other end.

Maggie was shivering as if every door and window in the house had suddenly been thrown open. Arms crossed over her breasts, she stared unseeingly at the small scar on the wall caused by the back of the chair being constantly shoved against it. She refused to allow some cretin to upset her. She had lived through far worse crises in her life and come through them. She could weather this one.

"Maggie?"

Just because some jerk got his kicks from frightening women who lived alone—just because she had blown her budget for the next six months on a set of new tires, that didn't mean she was going to fall apart.

"Maggie, dammit—!"

Just because this person had invaded her home until she was afraid to answer her own phone didn't mean he had won. She was a lot tougher than her mother gave her credit for being; she took after her father's side of the family, and Duncans did *not* go down without a fight.

She wasn't even aware of the tears streaming down her face until she heard the great gasping sob that tore from her throat, and she bent over, trying to hold back the tears with her fists.

A flurry of rain beat a tattoo against the side of the house as Sam gathered her into his arms. Maggie turned her face into his shirt collar, clutching his shoulders as he rocked her gently to and fro. "There, honey, whatever it is, we can handle it. I'll help you, you know that. Maggie, Maggie, please don't cry so hard, you'll make your throat sore."

"I never cry. I haven't cried in years."

"Mmm-hmm," was all he said.

The light flickered, blinked off, came on again, and went off and stayed. Maggie's face was buried in his neck, her eyes evidently shut tightly. Sam gazed over her head at the darkness surrounding them and swore silently. Had he thought he could remain uninvolved? Hell, he hadn't stood a chance. He'd been involved since the first time he'd slammed into her, swinging along the beach in that outlandish canvas coat and hat. Women like Maggie Duncan didn't happen to a man but once in a lifetime. He wasn't sure yet if that was a curse or a blessing; all he knew was that ready or not, he was in it up to his ears.

She needed him. That was a beginning. After that... well, they'd just have to wait and see.

The sobs were becoming erratic by now. He continued to stroke her back, to rub his face against her hair, and to murmur the occasional word of comfort. Unfortunately, the need to reassure her was giving way to a far more pressing need. He was going to be pretty damned embarrassed if she happened to notice.

"It's all right, honey. There's nothing we can't handle together." She hated to have him see her cry; he could sense it by the way she kept trying to control her breathing. But then she'd hiccup and sigh, and another deep, shuddering sob would rack her body, and it was all he could do not to bawl, too. He'd never empathized with a woman this way before, and he wasn't sure he liked the feeling of being so vulnerable.

"Maggie, I think the power just went off."

A muffled hiccup was her only response. She felt as frail as a reed in his arms, yet there was strength there, too. She smelled of honeysuckle and wood shavings, and he was increasingly aware of the pressure of her breasts against his chest and the growing tightness of his own loins. He told himself he was acting like the worst kind of opportunist, but it didn't help much.

"Maggie . . . honey, take a deep breath and hold it for a moment. It'll help you get over the hiccups." He wished he knew an equally simple cure for what ailed him. Actually, he knew of two, but the first was way out of line, and as for the second, he could hardly excuse himself long enough to take a cold shower.

"Okay, let's talk about it. Is it true that the sheriff knows who's been bothering you?"

Sniffing, Maggie began searching her pockets for a tissue. She didn't even seem to notice when Sam dropped his arms and stepped back. "I was just bluffing," she said, smearing her wet cheeks with her sleeve.

"Then you don't really know?"

"If I did, don't you think I'd have done something about it by now?"

They were facing each other—he thought—in the pitch-black room. Outside, the rain was beating down in earnest now. Sam was beginning to feel slightly disoriented. "Right now I think we'd better see about locating an oil lamp or at least a candle. Then I think you'd better tell me everything that's happened."

"And what *I* think is that I'd better go crank up the generator." Her voice was husky but quite firm, and Sam could tell she was already backing away from the brief closeness that had sprung up between them.

He wasn't going to allow her to get away with it. Whether she knew it or not, Sam Canady had staked his claim. He had approximately two weeks to convince her that they belonged together and at the moment, he hadn't the foggiest notion of how he was going to go about it. "I've got a flashlight. Just tell me what to do, where the switch is, and I'll start it up."

"I'd have to go show you, so I might as well do it my-self. I suppose you could come along and hold the light."

It wasn't going to be easy, he warned himself. She had independence down to a fine art. But that hard outer shell had begun to crack, and it was up to him to see that it didn't close up again.

Maggie could hear Sam bumping into furniture as she crossed the room to where she kept her rain gear. "Watch the stove pad, it lifts up on the corner," she said, just as he swore long and loud.

Stepping into her boots, she reached for the yellow slicker and matching sou'wester. As an afterthought, she felt for the dish towel and stuffed it into her pocket. The spark plugs would be wet with condensation.

"Where the devil did I put the flashlight," Sam grumbled. "Where are you? I can't see a thing."

"I'm right—"

She turned toward the sound of his voice, but before she could finish speaking, his outstretched hand found her plastic-covered breast. He snatched it back immediately, and she grinned in the darkness. Poor Sam. She hadn't been so distraught that she'd missed what had happened to him when he'd been comforting her. Not wanting to embarrass him, she'd pretended not to notice.

Sam was a special sort of man, strong and caring, in spite of his crusty exterior. Maybe she'd sensed that about him from the beginning. Maybe that was the reason she'd taken such pains to keep her distance. It had been an in-stinctive measure of self-defense on her part, even before she'd discovered that he had a wife. Having been married to a man who didn't know the meaning of the word fidel-ity, she wasn't about to get involved with another wom-an's husband.

"Got it," Sam said from close by. "It was in my coat pocket. Ready to go?"

It took twenty minutes and one bruised knuckle to get the four cylinders chugging away, but they managed. Sam took her hand to steady her as she stepped down out of the shed, and then he fastened the door behind them. "You're sure you worked for a brokerage house and not a garage?" he teased. "So, how come I got to change all four tires by myself?"

"Because you insisted on playing the macho role. A woman's place is in the kitchen, remember?"

"I'm beginning to think you don't fit the stereotype, Maggie Duncan."

"That's probably the nicest thing you've ever said to me, Sam Canady. Actually, *you* do."

"I do what?"

"Fit the stereotype. The married man vacationing alone, checking things out." For a moment she thought she'd gone too far. Under the single bulb that hung from a wire outside the shed, he looked grim and even a bit threatening.

"I guess I didn't mention that I'm no longer a husband. Laurel was killed in an accident New Year's Eve almost three years ago. She was pregnant at the time."

For a long time she could only stare at him. There was no way he could be lying to her. Not a man like Sam. She might not like him very much—or perhaps the trouble was, she liked him *too* much—but she would bet her life on his integrity.

"Sam, I'm sorry. I don't know what to say."

"There's nothing that needs saying. We're neither of us kids. I'm just sorry if I gave you the wrong idea. It wasn't intentional." But wasn't it? Hadn't he deliberately been throwing up a barrage because he'd sensed even then that this woman was getting too close?

He honestly didn't know. "Sooner or later, we need to talk, Maggie, but first come by my place. I have something I want to show you."

Maggie wasn't at all sure she wanted to take the risk. When she'd thought he was married and simply looking for dalliance, that was one thing. After four years, she'd become fairly adept at dealing with that sort of approach, even finding a certain degree of amusement in some of the more outrageous lines. But a Sam who was single, who'd been hurt, who was possibly as vulnerable as she was . . . that was another matter altogether.

"So? I promise you, I didn't bring along a portfolio of etchings."

"If it's not art, and your plumbing's not stopped up, then—oh, wait a minute! Don't tell me you finally managed to get a fire lit."

He laughed, and after a moment, she joined in. It was as if both of them were grateful for a release from the tension that had started with her phone call and ended with his revelation.

"You'll see," Sam said smugly, leading her up onto his back stoop. The roof extended halfway over it, and he stepped out of his muddy boots, leaving them under its shelter. In the narrow beam of the flashlight, Maggie noticed a few remaining pieces of wet driftwood. None of them would have made a decent base. None of them would burn, either, but he'd probably already discovered that for himself.

"Over here," he said, ushering her into his kitchen. It was cold and dark, and there was a musty, unfamiliar odor. "Oh—!" Sam uttered an obscenity, then said apologetically, "Sorry. I seem to have stepped in something."

"Sam, what's that noise?"

"Easy, sport, it's only me. I've brought home company," he replied, only Maggie didn't think he was talking to her. He placed the flashlight on the table so that its beam gave off a feeble glow, shrugged out of his wet slicker and slung it across a chair. "Let me help you with your coat. Second thought, maybe you'd better keep it on—it's kind of chilly in here."

"Chilly? It's arctic!"

"Come over here closer to the stove."

"Sam, I've got news for you. You have to build a fire in one of these things before it will put out any heat."

"Later," he said dismissively. "There—in the box on the floor. How do you like 'em, aren't they something?"

If he'd suddenly presented the crown jewels on a white satin pillow, he couldn't have sounded more proud. While Sam located the nub of a candle and finally managed to get it lit, Maggie stared down at the wriggling boxful of nondescript fur and pleading brown eyes. Her jaw dropped. "What—who—where did you get *that*?"

"They adopted me." His teeth gleamed palely in the gloom.

Later, Maggie thought that if she'd had to list all the emotions that had raced through her at the sight of that pathetic animal and her brood of fat, sleepy babies, she'd have been hard pressed. Sam stood beside her, one arm draped over her shoulder. It struck her that they might well be proud parents beaming down into a bassinet and she nearly shamed herself with tears for the third time in less than twenty-four hours.

Mostly as a defense, Maggie blurted out the first thing that came to mind. "Sam, she's the ugliest wretch I've ever seen in my life."

She might have known he'd get huffy. "Well, hell—you'd be pretty strung out, too, if you were trying to raise a family on your own, scrounging for food, trying to keep a roof over your head. She's a good mother, and that's more important than any beauty contest."

Maggie swallowed the suspicious lump in her throat. "Well...I suppose it's hard to judge, considering she's half-buried under all those wriggling little fur-balls. I count three, is that right?"

Somewhat mollified, he nodded. "Two little boys and a girl."

"Do you think she'd mind if I held one?"

"Introduce yourself to her first. Let her smell your hand."

"I think it smells like gasoline and iron rust."

"She's not particular—are you, sweetheart?" He knelt beside the box, held out his own hand, and when the bitch stretched her scrawny neck up to receive his caress, he grinned up at Maggie as if he'd just been awarded a medal.

"Let me do it." Maggie knelt, too, edging him aside.

"She might have a few fleas."

"So, what's a few fleas between friends?" Shyly, she introduced herself to the lady of the box. "Hi there, Brownie."

"Her name is Princess."

"How do you know? I don't see any name tag."

"Because I named her, that's why. Anyway, she's not brown."

"You're right. In fact, I think I may have discovered my red wolf. All right, Princess, if the name fits, wear it." Privately, she thought the poor old mutt lent new meaning to the word *ugly*, not that she would dream of mentioning such a thing again in Sam's presence. Funny how protective he was considering how long he'd had them. Another facet of his complex personality slid into place, but there were still a lot of blanks.

"How'd you find them?" she asked.

He explained briefly, seeing no reason to embellish the facts with an account of his brief...reservations. "The one with the black rings around his eyes tried to drag me under the Rover single-handed. I've kind of got a soft spot for him. I call him Popeye."

"You've got a soft spot for all of them," Maggie teased.

"Hey, you're not allergic, are you?"

"Not that I know of. I haven't had a dog since I was nine years old, but I didn't have any problems then."

"These are my first," Sam admitted almost shyly, and Maggie edged closer to him, so that their thighs and shoulders were touching. She felt a rather startling urge to put her arms around him and cradle his head against her breast.

"I'm sure you'll be very happy together," she murmured, trying to picture him showing up at home with this flea-bitten menagerie. The bitch was an undistinguished shade of reddish gray, her wiry hair matted with all manner of filth. Her neck was too thin for her head, and her ears were the wrong size and shape for her nose—or vice versa. None of her features seemed designed to go together. She was totally without charm, her only saving grace being that she seemed miserably aware of it.

As for the pups, they were a mixed batch, all three resembling their mother to some degree. "Sam, they're cold. Look how she's shivering."

"Who isn't? One of those little devils piddled on the floor while I was gone, and I waded through it in my sock feet."

"You're obviously not equipped to look after them," she said, sliding her hand in among the hot, squirming bodies. "I suppose I'd better take them over to my place."

"Not on your life, lady. Princess and her babies are my responsibility and they'll stay my responsibility."

Maggie lifted one of the pups up to cradle it against her neck. "Sam, be sensible. At least I've had some experience with dogs. I know something about caring for them." Her single experience had been Hamlet, the elderly Scottie her Uncle Henry had given her when she was nine. The dog had been given to him by someone else, and it had been a case of mutual dislike. Uncle Henry had been set in his ways and so had Hamlet.

Maggie had adored them both. "Have you fed her? A nursing mother needs twice the usual amount of food." She knew that much from the books she'd read while she was pregnant.

"Sure I've fed her. SpaghettiOs and ravioli, a can of each. Princess doesn't care for tomato soup."

"Oh, for Pete's sake, she needs more than that!"

"Like what, for instance?" Even knowing he was on distinctly shaky ground, Sam didn't care to have his judgment questioned.

"Like—like *dogfood*!" Maggie searched her memory for any scraps of pet lore. The last livestock she had tended were the three old hens Jubal had kept for eggs. "She needs nursing mash!"

"Never heard of it," he dismissed. "Look, maybe you'd better put Sweetpea back with her mother for now. The Princess is getting upset."

"Sweetpea," Maggie muttered, cradling the puppy in her arms. "Princess. God, you really pick some names, don't you?"

At that moment the lights flickered back on. Blinking, Sam stared at the woman kneeling beside him, the tiny fur-ball lying contentedly on its back in her arms. Something soft and lethal hit him square in the solar plexus. *Maggie, Maggie, don't make me wait too long.*

Maggie nuzzled the pup. "Poor sweety, just because you got picked up by old Scrooge, that doesn't mean you're stuck with him. You can come home with Maggie, darling. Maggie's been wanting a big, strong watchdog just like you." She put Sweetpea back with her mother and picked up another one. "And you, too, Popeye."

"Aww, come on now, Maggie, they're too young to be moved. Besides, they're full of fleas. You don't want to get your house infested, do you? Tell you what, if you want one, I'll give you your pick of the litter before I leave, okay?"

Maggie reached for the third one, who was still firmly attached to his supper at the moment. "If you haven't named this one yet, I'd like to call him Henry."

"Be my guest. From this moment on she'll be known as Henry."

"You mean Sweetpea is a boy?"

"I always thought he was in the comic strip. Are you telling me he was a girl?"

Laughing, Maggie leaned back against him for a moment. It was only the briefest of touches, merely a gesture of shared joy, shared amusement. But Sam's deep chuckle struck right through her, making her feel all warm and liquid inside. "He wore dresses, didn't he? I think Henry likes me, don't you?"

"Henry shows excellent judgment."

Covering the pleasure his words brought, she spoke brusquely. "Sam, they're too young to be weaned, and I'm pretty sure they need a place that's warm and dry.

Why don't I just take the lot of them over to my place. First thing tomorrow, I'll see about having them checked over by a vet. You don't want to be bothered by a pack of stray dogs.''

"If I didn't want to be bothered, I would've left them out in the rain.'' Under the Rover, in the shelter of the carport, actually, but he was in no mood to quibble.

"My place is a lot warmer. They need warmth.''

"It's raining. They'd get wet on the way over.'' Regardless of what he felt for Maggie, the more she argued, the more determined Sam was to hang on to his dogs. He had found them. They were his responsibility. And nobody, not even Maggie Duncan, was going to waltz in here and take away the whole boxload.

The light flickered feebly, threatening to go off again at any moment. Sam got to his feet, and so did Maggie. The tension that vibrated between them concerned far more than a box full of dogs. Sam knew this. So did Maggie. As deep hazel eyes blazed into warm amber ones, Princess and her brood were all but forgotten.

Maggie had never been more aware of the differences between a man and a woman. Between this man and all other men she had ever known. It was more than just his wild gray curls and tanned face, the rugged, slightly irregular features. It had little to do with his height or the breadth of his shoulders and the narrowness of his hips.

It had everything to do with the essential man. A man who was stubborn to a fault, who worked hard to keep from exposing his sensitive nature. A man whose instincts were to protect those weaker or less fortunate. To protect even Maggie, whom he hardly knew.

A man she could all too easily fall in love with, Maggie admitted with a sinking feeling.

"The dogs were found on my property," she persisted. "That makes them my responsibility."

"Forget it. You said yourself that the only cottage you own is the one you live in. As holder of a month's lease, I—"

"Lease! You paid rent, you didn't sign any lease!"

"As the lawful occupant of the residence where said mongrels currently reside, I hereby claim—"

"Claim, my foot!" Maggie leaned forward, realizing her mistake too late as she caught a drift of Sam's aftershave mingled with the musky smell of the dogs. "You can't even keep them warm! You don't even know what to feed them!"

"I can learn, dammit! If you're such a hotshot at taking care of everything, how come you're stuck out here all alone in the back of beyond with four flat tires, a yard full of garbage and no electricity? Answer me that!"

Her head went up. Had she thought of him as sensitive? He was as sensitive as a warthog. "I no longer have four flat tires—"

"Thanks to me!"

"I would have managed," she said grimly. "Furthermore, I do *so* have electricity, and there's not a scrap of garbage in my yard!"

"No? And I suppose you didn't get a phone call from some creep that scared the pants off you?"

"That's none of your business. I can handle it."

"You can't handle—" And then it got to him. Watching her stand there, fists on her hips, eyes blazing at him, Sam groaned. "Maggie, Maggie, what am I going to do about you?"

Before she could reply, he reached for her and hauled her tightly against him, sealing off her protests with a kiss born of anger and concern and need. She felt so right in his arms, even when she was stiff as a board. He felt as if he'd been in a deep freeze for almost three years. Now, suddenly the ice was cracking and deep currents were beginning to flow again, washing away the accumulation of pain and emptiness and frustration.

"Maggie, I need you—God, I want you so much," he whispered hoarsely.

No more than she wanted him. Maggie held on tightly, feeling the tension in every muscle in his body, sensing the urgency. Feeling the same urgency herself. His mouth eased its pressure, sliding sensuously over hers, and the tip of his tongue traced the curving fullness of her lower lip. She could feel his need pulsating against her, triggering an answering need deep in the center of her being.

"Sam, this isn't smart," she protested weakly.

"Maybe not, but it's inevitable. It was inevitable the first time I saw you. The first time I heard some guy mention a place called Duncan's Neck on the Alligator River and thought to myself, that sounds like the sort of place where I could find what I need." His hand moved down her back, cupping her hips to hold her tightly against him. "Only I didn't know what it was I needed. I didn't know until I found it, Maggie."

She made a halfhearted effort to free herself, but he refused to release her. Instead, he led her into the living room, which was even colder and more uninviting than the kitchen, if that were possible. The cheap, brightly colored furnishings seemed to huddle forlornly around the cold wood stove, but neither of them cared. They saw only each other, heard only the incessant rain and the quick, shallow sound of their own breathing.

Springs protested as Sam lowered her down to the sofa, half covering her with his own body. He was warm and hard, and she was no longer aware of the cold. Maggie made one last effort. "Sam, I'm afraid to get involved with you." Her hands played over his shoulders, which felt like warm granite under the covering of his flannel shirt.

"Hush, love, there's nothing to be afraid of. Besides, it's too late to worry about that, we're already involved." He kissed her then, letting her know the full force of his hunger. His fingers were at the neck of her shirt, working at the buttons, and she wanted to tear off her clothes, to give him access to all of her. Just as she wanted to see him, to feel the beat of his heart under her palm, to kiss his flat nipples and feel them peak against her lips.

Too many layers, too many buttons. She could feel the rigid pressure of him against her abdomen, and her thighs parted instinctively. Dear God, she wanted him! She had never wanted any man so much, not even in the early days with Carlysle. How could it have happened so quickly? Why now? Why Sam?

Over the drone of the rain, the sound of their breathing was loud in the barren room. Sam buried kisses in the soft hidden parts of her neck, places that were covered by her hair. He kissed his way down the sensitive tendon at the side of her throat, causing ripples of shuddering pleasure to race through her.

"I want to see you," he whispered, sliding his hands under the top of her overalls. Even through the flannel, she could feel the heat of his mouth, the gentle bite of his teeth, and she groaned. "I want to make love to every inch of you until I lose consciousness, and then I want to wake up and begin all over again."

He had unfastened the brass button at her waist and slipped his hand through the opening, under her shirttail, to the smooth, warm hollow of her belly. He spread his fingers, touching her sensitive navel with one, and sliding under the lacy elastic of her underpants with another.

Maggie gasped. She felt herself melting, her pulse hammering in all the secret places of her body. If ever she was going to come to her senses, it had to be now. Another moment and it would be too late. For both of them.

"Sam, wait—please."

"Maggie, don't stop me now. You know you want it as much as I do." His voice was like the sound of tearing velvet.

"I'm not denying that. But Sam, there's something you don't know. There's a lot neither of us knows." This wasn't going right—how could she make him understand? "Look, all I'm saying is we need to talk first, to—"

"Talk! Maggie, what good does talking do? We always end up fighting. But the loving would be so good between us—I know it would. You know it too, don't you?" He hadn't moved. His hand was still splaying out over her naked skin. "Don't you, darling?" he whispered coaxingly.

"That's not the point." She tried to twist away, but there was no room.

Evidently, she'd gotten through to him. He withdrew his hand and sat up, leaving her feeling cold and exposed, as if she'd been stranded out on a reef alone on a cold winter night.

"All right then, Maggie, suppose you tell me what the point is."

Eight

―――

The point is" Maggie said. And then she sat up, rearranged her clothing and cleared her throat. "The point is..."

"The point is that you get your kicks out of teasing, not following through. Is that it, Maggie? Was that enough for you?"

She flinched as if he had struck her, and Sam had the grace to look ashamed. He knew Maggie better than that. She was too straightforward to play that sort of game. If she wanted a man, that man would know it. If she didn't, she'd make damned sure he got the message, loud and clear.

The trouble was, either she was sending out mixed signals, or he was reading them wrong. It was possible, he acknowledged, that he was just seeing what he wanted to see.

"I'm sorry, Maggie. That was way out of line. Look, you said we needed to talk, so I suggest we go over to your place where we won't risk getting pneumonia."

Maggie let out the breath she'd been holding. "And take the dogs? The rain's slacked off."

A reluctant smile broke the grimness of his face when the lights went off again with no warning. Now that they were no longer touching, he was feeling the cold, and Maggie was openly shivering. "I give up. You've obviously got the elements and the local power company under your thumb. You may as well take the dogs, too. I should have known I wouldn't stand a chance against the resident witch—ah, make that wizard."

Maggie risked reaching out for him in the darkness. Encountering an arm, she squeezed. "Sam, I'd feel guilty being warm and cozy over there with Princess and the royal three, thinking of you all alone over here freezing in the dark."

"If you're offering me an electric blanket, then no thanks, unless you happen to have a kerosene model."

"There's a spare bedroom going to waste over at my house. It was Jubal's. Your power could be off for days— I'm pretty low on their priority list—but there's no point in your being cold and waterless over here when you can just as easily share my resources, such as they are. It won't take any more wood to cook for two of us."

He was silent for so long she was beginning to regret her impulsive offer. Then he said, "I appreciate that. Don't any of the other places have their own generator?"

Maggie breathed a sigh of relief. She'd been afraid he would take her offer the wrong way. Or refuse it out of misplaced pride. "A.B. has enough to worry about, filling the renters in on how to use the appliances, without that added complication. Not to mention expense."

"Funny, I don't remember his taking much time to explain about dampers and what to do when there's no wood."

Maggie felt around for the buttons on her shirt, securing them all the way up to her neck. "He probably took one look at you and decided you knew more about it than he did."

"Thus proving how deceptive looks can be, huh?" The springs creaked as he got to his feet.

"I didn't say a word," Maggie said self-righteously, but then she spoiled it with a soft giggle. She couldn't see him, but she could still feel his nearness. It felt good.

"Maggie, are you sure? I'll try not to be obtrusive."

"You've been obtrusive since the first day you showed up here. I suspect you're too old to change."

"I don't know which to take offense at first, the crack about being obtrusive, or being old," he said, and she laughed again, with a sense of having narrowly missed stumbling into quicksand.

"Let's start bundling up the babies. I can hardly wait to get them home," she said, and he let it slide, the remark about getting them home. "First thing tomorrow, I'll start checking around for a vet."

While Sam settled Princess and her brood in their new quarters, Maggie lit the fire in the living-room stove and opened the door to Jubal's old room. There were two more bedrooms upstairs, but the second floor had been closed off for years.

She'd brought out a box of wood shavings and sawdust for bedding instead of the quilt Sam had used. That would need airing for a week and then washing before it would be fit to use again.

Hearing Sam's deep murmurings as he bedded the dogs down in a corner of the kitchen made her smile. She'd forgotten how nice it was to have someone she cared for in the house.

So much for independence, she thought wryly as she shook out a thick blanket and spread it over the old sleigh-frame bed. The handmade Honduras mahogany bed and dresser had belonged to her grandmother. They were the only really nice pieces in the house.

In the act of dusting the dresser top with her sleeve, she paused and smiled. Sam was singing. Surprisingly, he had a rich, powerful baritone. In fact, it might have been considered excellent if only he could carry a tune. She propped an elbow on the dresser, smiling dreamily as he cheerfully butchered one of her favorite Beatles songs.

The phone rang, and he broke off. Maggie stiffened, on guard in case it was her vandal again.

"Want me to get it?" Sam called out. Her one phone was in the kitchen, and that had only been installed after she'd come to live there.

"Please?" If it was the anonymous caller again, maybe hearing a man's voice would discourage him. At least he'd know she was no longer alone here.

"It's a man. Says he's your cousin," Sam called out, but Maggie had reached the kitchen doorway by that time.

"It's Deke," she said, reaching for the phone.

Sam listened unashamedly. He wasn't about to leave her alone talking to someone who might or might not be who he claimed to be.

"Oh, hello, Deke," Maggie said, bracing her hips against the table and crossing her arms over her chest.

"Mary Margaret, where the dickens have you been? I've been trying for the past hour to get you."

"I've been in and out," she said noncommittally. It was none of his business where she'd been, but that never seemed to occur to Deke Elkins.

"I heard over the radio that there was a power outage all along that section of the river."

"I have Jubal's old generator, remember? Deke, if you just called to check on me, then thanks—I'm fine. I appreciate your concern, but I've got a million things to do, so if you'll—"

"Who answered the phone?"

She was tempted to tell him it was her latest lover, but with Sam standing there openly listening to every word, she didn't have the nerve. "A friend," she said instead. Which was no less than the truth.

"Anyone I know?"

"I doubt it. Look, Deke, if there's nothing else—"

"M.M., there's a nice new condo going up out on the beach. I could work a deal for you if you sign up now. I worry about you over there all by yourself. There's the prison not too far away..."

"It's miles from here. The local raccoons are a greater threat. I'm going to trap one I know of and transport him to the landfill. He'll think he's died and gone to heaven."

"About that condo..."

"No thanks, I could never afford it, Deke."

"Well, seeing as how you're family, and family has to stick together, I could offer you a good price for Jubal's place. Besides, you're bound to have plenty of investments left."

"What I have or don't have left is no concern of yours, cousin. And now, I really do have to go. I have houseguests."

"Houseguests! Mary Margaret, who—"

"Oh, and do you happen to know a realtor named H. J. Wilkerson?"

There was a moment of silence on the other end. And then the single word, "Why?"

"Because he came to see me the other day," Maggie replied, enjoying the feeling of having momentarily knocked her cousin off his chrome-plated perch.

"I'd advise you to let me handle any dealings you have concerning the property. Wilkerson's notorious for buying up land at bargain prices and then turning it around to make a killing for himself and his little group of cohorts."

"Ohhhh," she said softly, thoroughly enjoying herself by now, "and of course, that's considered unethical."

"Now, Mary Mar—"

She didn't wait for more, but gently replaced the phone in its cradle. Her shoulders lifted and fell in a heavy sigh, and she turned to find Sam studying her intently. "You, too?"

"Me, too, what?" He lifted one of the dark brows that contrasted so strikingly with his silvery hair.

"You, too, the Inquisition. Deke thinks that just because he's my only kin south of Boston, he has the right to run my life for me."

"I take it he doesn't approve of your living out here alone?"

"In a nutshell."

"Do your parents?"

"Do my parents approve?" Sighing again, she picked a puppy out of the box and cuddled him under her chin. "In case you hadn't noticed, I'm hardly a child."

"I'd noticed. All the same, I can understand their being concerned. I've only known you a couple of weeks, and I'm concerned about you."

Maggie put the puppy back with his mother. Princess had eaten two fish cakes and a bowl of cereal when they'd first arrived, and now she seemed nicely settled in. "Don't be. I appreciate your concern, but I don't need it. I've been taking care of myself for years."

With a sibilant oath, he moved to her side, clamped his hands on her shoulders, and silently dared her to look him in the eyes. "You're the one who wanted to talk, remember? So stop freezing me out. The minute I get too close, you start icing over, and I know damned well it's not because you're indifferent to me! If you don't want me here, then say so. If you're not interested in finding out what it is we have between us, all you have to do is tell me to back off. I'm no masochist."

Here was her opportunity to get rid of him. All she had to do was tell him to leave her alone, and he would do just that.

And she couldn't. "If you've mangled my shoulders to your satisfaction, I'd like a chance to try and explain something."

Releasing her, he apologized, swore, and apologized again. It was all Maggie could do not to throw her arms about him. "Now that I have the microphone, I'm not sure where to start."

"At the beginning?"

"Let's see . . . I was a long baby, seven pounds, three ounces and twenty-two inches from the point of my head to the tip of my wrinkled—"

"Maggie," Sam warned quietly.

"I was an indifferent scholar except in art and math. Weird combination, but it worked for me. First a broker, now a sculptor—actually, sort of a glorified whittler, but—"

"Back up to the broker business. I can't picture you anywhere but here, but I always had a feeling you didn't quite fit here, either."

She sighed. They were sitting down, having pulled the chairs around so that they both had a view of the dogs. "Half of me belongs here, half of me doesn't know where it belongs anymore. Maybe no one ever does."

"What about your husband—was he a broker, too?"

"An attorney. I met Carlysle when I was just getting established. You see, my father is something of an institution in financial circles, so naturally I was expected to succeed brilliantly. Who knows, maybe I would have in time. Carr was evidently impressed enough to marry me, and things like success meant a lot to him. Coffee?"

"What?"

Needing space to breathe, she got up and ran water in the pot, dumped in half a cup of ground coffee, and set it on the stove. Then she got out two cups and the can of milk.

"I guess it was what Jubal called the Duncan backbone that kept me going. Carr and I were competitive, although that didn't occur to me at the time. If he got a plum of a case, I had to match him and vice versa. It was almost like a game, only after a while, I'd had enough. I wasn't sleeping well—Carr was spending a lot of time away from home. Tension used to get me at the back of my neck until I was as stiff as a board, and I lived on Maalox. I was named junior VP, and Father was over the moon. Carr said the firm of Dean, Upham Ross had more VPs than they did potted plants, but if it made me happy... Sam, why am I telling you all this mess? It's nothing to do with us."

"Indulge me. We have a lot of catching up to do." Sam pulled her chair closer to his and marveled at her gracefulness as she lowered herself and extended a foot toward the dogs' bed. God, she was so lovely it almost hurt to look at her. Carr. Carlysle Leseur. The jerk sounded like some fancy hairdresser, but evidently he'd been man enough to win her. She would never have married a man she didn't love, not his Maggie.

The acid that burned in his veins was not difficult to identify. He was jealous. Jealous as hell, and he hadn't even been jealous of the man who had fathered Laurel's baby.

Which only confirmed something he had suspected already.

"And then I got pregnant," Maggie said baldly.

Sam groaned, and she looked up at him curiously, noticing for the first time the lines of stress around his mouth, the bleakness of his eyes. "Go on," he said, his voice rough with barely controlled emotion.

"We hadn't planned on having children—at least we hadn't discussed it, but I discovered that I really wanted my baby. I think it must have been then that I began to realize how little satisfaction I was getting out of either my career or my marriage. I was tired of pushing, tired of never having any time for the two of us, much less myself alone, tired of never being able to entertain without having some pressing business reason for doing it."

She sighed. "I suppose I was just tired, period."

"And Carlysle? How did he react to the news?" Sam prompted when she lapsed into a silence that threatened to go on and on.

"He said I had to...get rid of it. He didn't want it. He said we couldn't afford it." She laughed harshly then, and the sound cut right through him. "A family of four could have lived for a year on what the pair of us brought home in any given month, and we couldn't afford one tiny baby. I'd even planned to nurse her.''

Sam almost dreaded what he was going to hear. God knows he understood guilt, and compared to her, he'd had no basis at all. If she'd gotten rid of her baby and now regretted it, he was going to have a hell of a time convincing her that she'd punished herself long enough. But for her sake—for both their sakes—he knew he was going to try. No woman deserved to be banished for life for a decision she'd made under great emotional pressure.

"Carlysle threatened to leave me. He said I had to choose between him and the baby. I chose our baby, and he moved into a hotel. After that, things got pretty hectic. I had to make other living arrangements, and that took time. The market was going wild—up one day, plummeting the next. I had clients after me day and night, wanting reassurance, wanting to know—''

She took a deep breath, swallowed hard, and brushed a few dog hairs off her jeans. "Breaking up a marriage is an awfully messy business," she said quietly. "Time consuming. My parents weren't much help. Mother was sure I was making a big mistake, my father was mostly concerned about whether or not I could keep up at work. In the end, I guess it was all too much. My blood pressure skyrocketed, and I landed in the hospital, and I...lost the baby.''

The pot on the stove boiled over, masking the aroma of wet dog with burned coffee. After a while, Maggie said calmly, "By the time I was able to go back to work, I discovered that I didn't want to. The Dow Jones could have doubled or bottomed out, and I wouldn't have cared. My divorce was in progress. Of course, by then I'd discovered that Carr hadn't let marriage cramp his style to any noticeable degree. He'd kept a mistress on the side, and he'd cheated on both of us. I decided I'd had enough, so I resigned, moved in with Jubal, and I've been here ever since."

She looked around with a brilliant smile that never quite reached her eyes. "So—there you have it. The tiresome tale of a woman's rotten judgment. I spent half my life preparing for a career I didn't want, married a man I couldn't keep, and lost the only thing of value I ever possessed. Can you wonder why I keep a low profile these days?"

"Nothing ventured, nothing lost?"

"More a case of knowing your assets and liabilities." Her smile faded, but a slow warmth began to kindle in her eyes.

Sam stirred himself to remove the coffeepot from the range. He held it under the faucet and allowed a trickle of cold water to trail down the side, and then waited a moment before pouring it. "If I had some brandy, I'd sweeten it up a tad. All I've got is a bottle of Jim Beam over at the house, but I'll get it if you need it."

"Do I look that wrung out?"

"You look beautiful. You've always looked beautiful, even when you were spittin' mad at me for trespassing on your beach and stealing your driftwood."

"You knew?"

"You made it pretty obvious," Sam said, adding just the right amount of canned milk to her cup before wrapping her cold fingers around it.

"Sorry. I suppose I've gotten pretty territorial over the years."

"Ever consider moving away—or sharing?"

She gazed into the depths of her coffee. "Occasionally I wonder if I could still function in Boston. I've never been really tempted to find out, but as for sharing, I share the Neck every summer with hordes of fishermen, mostly male, mostly decent enough—sometimes obnoxious. I can function well enough to deal with whatever A.B. sends my way."

"Including me?"

She tilted a grin his way. "Including you. I figure you won't last out your allotted time. You're not exactly a roaring success when it comes to roughing it, are you?"

"I could learn. Maybe we could split the difference—I learn to tolerate the Neck, and you try Durham on for size."

Maggie felt her heart trip into double time. "Sam, don't say things you don't mean. If you want to sleep with me, then that's one thing, but don't try to dress it up as something it's not. That's not fair to either of us."

"What makes you think I don't mean it?"

She sipped her coffee and grimaced while Sam waited for her answer. She'd got herself into this mess by inviting him over and then unloading on him. There was no graceful way out of it. "Are you saying you're in love with me?" she asked, which was about as graceless as you could get.

By the time Sam opened his mouth to reply, Maggie was wishing she could crawl under the linoleum. "Forget I said that. *Please.*" She could imagine how he must be feeling. As panic-stricken as she was, probably.

"Maybe I don't want to forget it. Maggie, there's something going on between us and we both know it."

"Propinquity?" she suggested hopefully.

He grinned, but his eyes were shadowed, impossible to read. "Hardly. Neither one of us was exactly thrilled to be trapped here with the other, but that didn't stop it from happening. Did it, Maggie?"

Having blundered so badly before, she wasn't about to admit to anything. Where was all that coolness under fire she had earned the hard way?

"Does the thought of getting involved with a man again bother you?"

"Bother me? It terrifies me. We don't even know each other, not really."

"Knowing takes time. If it will help shorten the process, maybe I should level with you about my marriage. I don't like to fail at anything—that was a failure almost from the start."

Maggie could tell how much it was costing him to speak of it. Sam was essentially a private person, as was she. One of the few things they had in common.

"I wasn't in love with my wife. I was fond of her—she was young and strikingly beautiful. She was also pregnant with another man's child. I married her because I was lonely and Laurel needed someone. The father of her baby was already married, and her parents weren't exactly the understanding type." He waited, and when she said nothing, he didn't know whether to shut up or go on. Maybe she really didn't give a damn. Maybe...

Maggie reached across the table and covered his hand with her own. "Thank you for telling me, Sam. Laurel chose wisely. You'd have made a wonderful father."

Inordinately pleased, he said, "I'd hardly say wonderful. Adequate, though. I think I could've managed adequate."

"Of course, you'd have spoiled a child rotten. Which reminds me, maybe we'd better let the Princess out again for a last run. Does she need anything else to eat? A bedtime snack?"

"Now who's trying to spoil her?"

Holding her hands palms outward, she pantomimed innocence. "You do the honors, then, while I shower. I'll save you some hot water."

She needed to move about. Being close to Sam Canady was rather frightening. Exhilarating, but frightening. Like driving too fast. Like racing downhill on a steep slope.

"Thanks. Speaking of spoiling," Sam said with a grin as he opened the back door for the dog.

She was already in bed when she heard the shower cut off some time later. She'd purposely skimped on her own shower, knowing the limited capacity of her hot-water heater. Sam deserved the luxury more than she did.

He rapped on her door and stuck his head in before she could reply. "Maggie, do I open a window, or what? Your house is tighter than mine."

"Suit yourself."

"Oh. Okay." He lingered, and she looked at him inquiringly. She'd left the living-room light on for him, and it shone across one corner of the foot of her bed.

"Must be like sleeping on a pillow. What happens when you bottom out?"

"By then you're asleep, so it doesn't matter."

"I've never slept in a feather bed."

"A lot of people haven't. Jubal's bed is hard, but at least you'll be warm."

"I know where I'd be a lot warmer," he said, and Maggie shifted restlessly. As if she hadn't followed his every movement since he'd come in from letting Princess out for a run. As if she hadn't pictured him standing under her shower, the clear plastic curtain tucked into the old claw-footed bathtub revealing the size and shape of his body, if not the details.

As if she hadn't imagined the details.

"Sam, did you want to say something? It must be almost midnight."

After a few moments, he said, "I guess I just wanted to say good-night."

"Good night, Sam."

And then he strode into the room, and she could see he was wearing a pair of jeans and nothing else. "Dammit, Maggie, you can't mean that! How do you expect me to sleep knowing you're lying here on the other side of the wall? Don't you know how much I want you? Don't you care?"

She didn't wait until her courage failed her. Spreading the covers aside with one sweep of her arm, she said, "Come to bed, Sam."

Nine

———

Sam stared at her for what seemed an eternity, seeing everything he'd ever wanted or hoped to see in her eyes. Then, waiting only long enough to shed his jeans, he came to her. His hair was still damp from the shower, and he smelled of toothpaste, a woodsy after-shave, and her honeysuckle soap. He was beautiful.

"Maggie, are you sure?"

He stood beside the bed, light from the room beyond highlighting the hair on his chest. It was dark, like his eyebrows, not gray. He had the body of a man in his early prime, except that it had probably taken years to hone it down to the lean efficiency suggested by the hard sinews and flat, muscular planes. His face was in shadow, and Maggie reached out and turned on the small lamp beside her bed. She wanted to see more of him.

She wanted to see all of him. "I'm sure." She smiled up at him from the snug hollow she had created in the bed, and it was all the assurance he needed. A moment later, feathery mounds billowed up around their two bodies, sealing them together in one small world.

Sam's face angled across her own, his mouth sipping like a butterfly until frustration set her fingers digging into his shoulders. Then, with an incredibly light touch, he traced the line between her lips with the tip of his tongue, lifting his head to smile down at her. She went wild with wanting. All pretense of restraint flew out the window and she wriggled out of her gown, wanting to touch every inch of his warm strength at once. A small sound, somewhere between a groan and a whimper, escaped her, and as if it were a catalyst, Sam buried his face in her hair, holding her so tightly she couldn't breathe.

"Maggie, Maggie, what magic herbs did you sprinkle over those collard greens? I swear I've never known anything to hit this hard with no warning." His jaw, rock hard but freshly shaven, dragged over her cheek as he found her lips and parted them with his own. It was even worse than she'd feared. His tongue thrust boldly inside, claiming her, inflaming her with urgent need.

If she hadn't been certain before, she knew now that she would never get enough of this man, of the taste and the feel of him. She wanted all of him—his mind, his body, his soul. The overwhelming compulsion to possess him was so powerful it was frightening.

What am I doing here? she thought desperately. They had nothing at all in common, they fought at the drop of a hat. Why had she poured out all that wretched past business? He'd asked—well, something—she couldn't remember, but he certainly hadn't asked for her life story. Like a lovesick adolescent, she'd wanted him to know everything there was to know about her, and to love her in spite of it. If that wasn't a sign she was losing touch with reality, she didn't know what was. Her mother had warned her that living alone could have a strange effect on a woman.

"Maggie? Where are you? Darlin', come back—I need you here with me," Sam whispered.

She swallowed hard, staring over his right shoulder. When he lifted his head to gaze down at her, she reluctantly met his eyes, knowing it was too late to back out now.

"Don't scare me like that, love. If you aren't ready, I can wait. Only don't go too far away—don't go where I can't follow." His hands were gentle on her face, and his mouth—had she ever thought it harsh? It was Sam's mouth, Sam's smile, with that unique little twist at the corners. She loved every sweet, sensuous curve.

Lifting her head from the pillow, she brushed him a kiss, and his arms tightened around her. "Sorry. It's been a while."

"For me, too, sweetheart. I don't want to rush you, but..."

She managed a throaty laugh that set the dark flames in his eyes to blazing higher than ever. "So rush me."

He needed no second urging. Fighting the feathery mounds of the bed, he rolled onto his back, bringing her over on top of him. Then he lifted her so that the tips of her breasts raked his chest. He groaned. "God, you're wonderful! I'm just so hungry for you I'm afraid I might hurt you."

"I won't break," she whispered breathlessly. He kissed her again, taking all she had to give and demanding more. And then he began nibbling a trail down the side of her throat, lifting her so that he could reach her breasts with his lips.

At the hot rasp of his tongue on her nipples, an explosion of pleasure so sharp it was almost pain streaked through her. Resting on her elbows, she curved her hands inward, combing her fingertips through the silky-crisp swirls on his chest until she encountered nubs of pinpoint-hard flesh.

A hard shudder racked his body. "Sweetheart, I'm on a short fuse, and it's burning fast." Reversing their positions, he threw back the covers, skimming his hands down her body. His legs stiffened against hers, their hair-roughened texture strangely exciting. She felt his manhood pulsing against her thigh, steel sheathed in velvet. Her arms tightened around him, her nails digging into the resilient flesh of his back. "Sam, please—I need you," she begged.

His voice was harsh, almost unrecognizable, as he fought to retain control. "Wait, love—give me a minute or it'll be all over before it even begins."

Wait! Hadn't she been waiting all her life for him? Now, having him here, holding him this way, his face pillowed on her breast so that the moist heat of his breath fanned her nipples, she felt the sweet bonds of pleasure begin to tighten around her before he had even entered her. Was it possible for any woman to want a man so much that she climaxed without his ever having touched her?

And then he touched her and she felt herself begin to leave the earth. His fingers had crept down over her abdomen, to the narrow pathway between her thighs, and he caressed her with a slow, sure touch that made her rock against him. His teeth closed gently over her nipple, and the feel of his tongue sent her flying even higher.

"Please—Sam, please," she whimpered frantically.

His mouth opened wider, suckling her with a slow, gentle hunger while his hands continued to work their spell. She wanted to touch him—she wanted to be a part of him—she couldn't find the words!

While he stroked her to the far edge of sanity, she traced a frantic pathway down his back, over the lean muscles of his hip, to his abdomen. There her fingers spread out, encountering the dense thicket she had only glimpsed briefly before he came down onto the bed beside her. "I want to touch you, too," she whispered.

She might as well have branded him with a red-hot iron. Every muscle in his body jumped when her hand brushed against his heated flesh, her fingers fluttering tentatively and then closing around him. He gave her a single moment, no longer, before he caught her wrist and dragged it up over her head. "Maggie, you're killing me, sweetheart. I can't take it!"

Hands trembling with urgency, he parted her thighs and fitted himself against her, his weight braced as he arched his body over hers. Breathing rapidly through parted lips, Maggie gazed up at the thrilling new harshness that rode his features. A flush stained his sharp, angular cheekbones, his eyes glittering like obsidian in the dim light of the rose-shaded lamp.

She cried out as he entered her. Collapsing, he buried his face in her throat. "Oh, God, Maggie, I'm sorry! It's been a long time, and I couldn't—" Groaning, he tried to pull back, but she wrapped her legs around him and held him there.

"No, please! Darling, you didn't hurt me. So sweet— just so wonderful—I'd forgotten, that's all." It was building again, that sweet hot pressure. She twisted her head helplessly, plowing her fingers through his hair and holding him to her. The flames were raging all around them, and she wanted to consume and be consumed. "Sam, please, I can't talk now. Just love me?"

He went still for a small eternity, burying himself in the deepest reaches of her body. Then his lips found hers, and he was kissing her with a wild desperation. She bit his lip, then drew it into her mouth and salved it with her tongue, and they clung together, fingers slipping on damp flesh. Someone had thrown back the covers, tossed both pillows to the floor. Maggie didn't remember doing that. Someone had also struck the lampshade a glancing blow, leaving it tilted to one side. Neither of them would have noticed if the roof had fallen in on top of them.

Sam began to thrust with slow precision. Once. Twice. And then he felt her tightening around him and all pretense and control was lost.

In the tangle of their limbs, he drove hard and furiously. Maggie felt the fire of life surge into her body a split second after she heard her own voice cry out in release. In that moment she knew that she had never loved anyone as much as she loved this man, nor had loving ever felt so utterly right.

Nor so hopelessly wrong. There were just too many reasons why they couldn't . . . why they shouldn't . . .

A consciousness that drifted just out of reach warned her that she was thinking with her emotions. Sooner or later, she assured it drowsily, she would engage her brain again. But not now. Not with her body still humming with pleasure. Not with Sam still holding her as if he would never let her go.

Eventually he managed to widen their nest to make a place for himself beside her, her head on his shoulder and one of her thighs trapped between his. Sometime later, he must have retrieved the covers, for Maggie remembered waking and thinking that she had never felt warmer or more sheltered in her life. Left to her, they would both have frozen. She couldn't have moved if her life had depended on it.

A few centuries passed and Maggie came partially awake, the sound of Sam's voice drifting to her in snatches. She smiled without opening her eyes.

"...pretty lady...breakfast," she heard him say. A man in a million. If she could have summoned the strength to speak coherently, she would have told him what she wanted for breakfast. Him.

"...make an appointment with the doctor today," he went on, and it occurred to her belatedly that neither of them had taken precautions, which, for a couple of supposedly mature adults, had been extremely irresponsible. Not that she regretted a single moment of it. She seriously doubted that Sam had come prepared for this sort of encounter. He probably took it for granted that she was protected, but after four celibate years, she'd all but forgotten the rules.

"...delouse you and fatten you up, and you'll be a real sweetheart."

Her eyes popped open and she sat up in bed. *Delouse her? Fatten her up?*

And then she remembered. Groaning, she eased one leg out of bed, then the other. Her thighs ached. That wasn't all that ached. She began to smile, and by the time she'd retrieved her flannel gown and pulled it on, she was grinning fatuously.

"Oh, you're awake."

"Mmmmm," she murmured, wishing he'd given her time to brush her hair and wash the sleep from her eyes before he'd brought her coffee.

"This isn't what you're used to, but I hope it'll do. I can't seem to get the hang of making that boiled stuff."

Maggie took the cup and sipped. It was delicious, and she told him so. You'd have thought she'd offered him the Nobel Prize for Caffeine Arts.

Beaming, he said, "I was looking in the pantry for a mop when I saw the coffee maker. Since I happen to be pretty familiar with that particular model, I took the liberty of cranking it up."

"Are the babies all right?"

"Yeah, only two puddles so far. I let Princess out for a run earlier, and she's back with them now, and Maggie," he hurried on without pause, "I want you to know that I meant everything I said."

She took another sip, trying to awaken her foggy brain. What had he said? That he was going to delouse her and fatten her up? But he'd been talking about the dogs... hadn't he?

"Last night, I mean," he added, seeing her frown.

The frown deepened as Maggie tried to recall anything he might have said last night. She could remember what they'd done, all right. Her whole body glowed with remembrance, but he hadn't really said all that much. Neither had she.

She smiled dreamily. "Me, too, Sam," she said, and had the pleasure of seeing a frown gather slowly between his dark eyes. "Now if you'll excuse me, I'd like a quick shower, and then I'll get us some breakfast. Ham, eggs and biscuits all right with you?"

A few moments later, she was singing in the shower. Her voice wasn't particular strong, nor even very melodious, but at least she could carry a tune. Which was more than she could say for some people she knew. It occurred to her as she rinsed the suds off her body that between them, she and Sam would make a wonderful singer.

Stepping out of the tub to stand before the clouded mirror, she smiled dreamily, remembering what else they made beautifully between them. The hazy oval of her face took on a decidedly rosy cast, and she laughed ruefully. She'd long since given up wishing she'd inherited the stable complexion of the Machapungo Indians on Jubal's mother's side of the family instead of the thin skin of her Scottish, Irish and English ancestors. She was a walking barometer, her skin registering the slightest emotional shift.

After slathering on moisturizer, she dressed in her best pair of jeans and a flattering yellow tank top, adding a railroad-striped overshirt and tying her hair back with a yellow-and-gray silk scarf, a remnant of her salad days. Hanging up her nightgown, she decided it was too bad she'd worn out the last of her Saks satin and lace and replaced it with Sears Roebuck flannel and terry cloth. But then, it had never occurred to her that something like this could ever happen.

Sam insisted on washing the dishes, so she picked up a dish towel and began drying and putting them away. "We split the chores fifty-fifty," he decreed. And then he grinned. "My bed's already made, how about yours?"

Maggie swatted him, which led to a game of chase, which ended up with her sprawled halfway across the kitchen table and him sprawled over her. "That's my elbow you just buttered," she accused, laughing up at him.

"You should've given me a chance to wash off the table before you attacked me. I'm afraid that calls for a pretty severe warning."

"Only a warning?" she taunted breathlessly. She could feel him hardening against her, see the telltale darkening of his eyes.

"Ma'am, it's my duty to warn you of what might happen if you take another swipe at my fanny with that dish towel."

"You're going to impose a fine?"

"Worse," he declared solemnly.

"Not incarceration! Please, Your Honor, I didn't know the towel was loaded."

"That's what they all say, but it's easy to see you're a hardened criminal."

Maggie's lips quivered in an effort to hold back laughter. "And it's easy to see that you're a hardened bailiff." She shifted her hips suggestively, delighting in the playful side of a man who had once struck her as stern and humorless.

"For shame, ma'am! Are you trying to influence the court? I'm going to have to put you away where you can't do any more harm."

"I happen to know of a lovely padded cell with iron bars at both ends." She batted her lashes with inexpert coyness.

"Hmmm...since you're so cooperative, I reckon I won't recommend solitary, but I'm afraid I'm going to have to search you just in case you happen to be concealing any more lethal linens."

As good as his word, Sam cupped the calf of her leg and began moving his hand slowly up the inside of her thigh. His fingertips trailed tantalizingly over her heated valley before following a lingering pathway up the button fly of her jeans to her waist. With a stern expression belied by a pair of wickedly dancing eyes, he slipped his hand under her shirt and moved it up to her breast. He was beginning to have serious difficulties with his breathing, but then, so was Maggie.

"Are you satisfied now that I'm harmless?" she managed to gasp.

"Yes, ma'am. About as harmless as a loaded shotgun. But just in case you're ever tempted to attack an unarmed man again, I'm going to give you a taste of what lies in store for you." With exquisite care, he toyed with her nipple until she felt the throb of her pulses in the deepest core of her body. She had the pleasure of knowing that he was every bit as aroused as she was. "Have you learned your lesson yet?"

"Yes, sir," Maggie replied, trying and failing to look suitably chastised. She had uncovered a brand new part of herself, and she discovered that she was enjoying it thoroughly.

Sam leaned over her threateningly, his breath stirring the hair at her temples. "You're sure? You don't look any too trustworthy to me."

"Word of honor, I'll give you a two-minute lead before I repair to the nearest linen closet to rearm myself."

It took only a moment, and then Sam burst out laughing. Sliding his arms under her shoulders, he lifted her up and cradled her against him, and Maggie had the pleasure of hearing his laughter through the warm, solid wall of his chest.

Princess, alarmed at the noise, began to whimper. Reluctantly, Sam stepped back, and Maggie slid off the table. "Unfortunately, my wicked little temptress, I made an appointment for this bunch to see a vet at ten-fifteen. We'll postpone judgment for now, okay?" He kissed her on each eyelid, on the tip of the nose, and then lingeringly on the mouth. Lifting his head so that his lips hovered over hers, he murmured, "I'm warning you, though—any more funny business with that dish towel, and it's back to the padded cell."

* * *

The vet recommended spraying both cottages thoroughly and then told them he was going to have to keep the dogs for two to three days. "With the bitch nursing, I'm going to have to use conservative means, but they've picked up just about every type of parasite going. It's been a real tough year for ticks and fleas. Hope we get a long, hard freeze pretty soon."

"But they'll be all right?" Maggie asked anxiously.

"The runt may be too far gone. I take it these were strays?"

Sam nodded gravely, and Maggie protested, "But Henry's the fattest one of all."

"I'll do what I can, Maggie. Give me a call tomorrow and I'll let you know how we're doing. I'm pretty sure the rest of 'em will be just fine once I get them cleaned up and cleared out, so to speak. You'll have to bring the pups back for follow-up shots."

After an emotional farewell, Sam and Maggie left the small animal clinic and strolled toward the Rover. "Look at us," Sam scoffed. "Can you believe we're carrying on this way over a pack of mutts we'd never seen before yesterday?"

Maggie shrugged. She was having enough trouble believing she could have fallen so hard for a man she'd known for such a short time. As for the dogs, that was easy to understand. Both she and Sam had needed something—or someone—to fill an emptiness in their lives. Having lost something precious, they had instinctively steered clear of any emotional involvement. Sheer self-protection. The survival instinct at work.

But time had passed, and old wounds had healed over. The puppies had come along, needing someone to care for them, and they were a safe way of filling a space in both their lives.

"I'm beginning to foresee a slight problem, Samuel." She leaned her hips against the sun-warmed door and squinted against the brilliant December sun. "D'you remember the story about King Solomon and the two women who both claimed the same baby?"

Sam gave her an oblique look as he fished a wad of keys from the pocket of his worn fatigues. "I wouldn't worry about it too much," he said, unlocking her door.

"I didn't say I was worried, I only said—"

"Don't anticipate problems, Maggie." He started the engine and wheeled expertly out of the small parking lot. "Things will work out, you'll see."

A little resentful of his high-handedness, she remained silent until they were almost home again, her thoughts a muddy riptide that threatened to drag her under. Last night should never have happened. She should have listened to that small voice that warned she'd better start thinking with her head instead of her heart. Or whatever part of her it was that persisted in misleading her where men were concerned

But it had happened. There was no turning back the clock. The trouble was, neither Sam nor she was ready to make a commitment. Physically they were great, but that just wasn't enough. His life was in Durham—hers was here. She'd made a place for herself, proved something to herself here in this wilderness, and she would be a fool to throw it all away.

Besides, he hadn't asked her to.

Just as they slowed down to turn off on the road to the Neck, a rusted, cut-down Falcon with a homemade truck bed jutting off the rear end came rattling out. Sam slammed on the brakes. "Who the hell is that idiot?" he asked as the other vehicle roared off toward Manteo.

"Oh, that's only Pogie. If he has a last name, I've never heard it."

"What's he doing on this road?"

She could tell the way Sam's suspicions were running. "If you're thinking Pogie is my vandal, forget it. He's been around forever. He runs traps in the woods—probably illegal, unlicensed and out of season. I suspect he harvests some of the lumber company's trees and sells cordwood when trapping gets slow, but he's been doing it for so long he's sort of an institution around here. They haul him off to court on a regular basis, but there's not much point in fining him—he doesn't have anything. And every time he winds up in jail, they have to fumigate it afterward."

Sam gave her a curious look. "And you're vouching for this character?"

"Sam, forget it. All Pogie wants is enough money to keep him in fortified wine and cigarettes. He'd never hurt anyone." In fact, at the moment she was rather grateful to the old reprobate for relieving the tension that had sprung up between them. Not that Sam had seemed aware of it. "How many bombs did we get? Do you think I need to set one off in the living room, or just the rooms where the dogs were?" she asked as he pulled up between the two houses.

"I'd do the living room, too, in case any crawled under the door. But not yet. First we pack."

"First we *what*?"

"Pack. Toothbrushes, shaving gear, a change of clothes, maybe. Just enough for overnight."

Impatiently, Maggie unclipped her shoulder harness and turned to stare at him. "Have I missed something?"

Draping his arm across the steering wheel, Sam sighed. "Honey, you don't think I'm going to let you hang around and breathe this stuff, do you? If it's guaranteed to kill ticks and fleas, it's not exactly health food. Trust me. I'm a chemical engineer."

"Oh, for pity's sake, everybody uses that stuff!"

"I'm not everybody. Okay, so I'm paranoid. Will you just listen to me, Maggie?"

The old Sam was clearly back in possession—stubborn, autocratic, too damned attractive for her comfort. Maggie clamped her lips shut, crossed her arms and waited, eyes snapping sparks. She would give him one minute, no more. If she weren't dangerously close to being in love with the man, she wouldn't have given him ten seconds. "So you're paranoid and that means I have to pack up and leave home. Just like that. No warning. Sam says jump and everybody jumps, right?"

One corner of his mouth twitched. "Something like that," he acknowledged.

"You've got forty-four seconds left."

"Wha-a-at? Come on, Maggie, you're being unreasona—"

"Thirty-two and counting."

"All right, dammit! What we're going to do is pack enough for overnight, put away everything that needs it, lock up, and bomb both places. I don't want Princess to get reinfested the minute she walks in the door, and I doubt if you'd enjoy coming down with fleabitus, either!"

Maggie was in no mood to appreciate his weak attempt at humor. Her emotions were all over the road. She felt edgy—spoiling for a fight. The truth was, she was growing more afraid by the minute. Afraid of what had happened to her already, and even more afraid of what would happen to her once Sam left.

"Don't you see, Maggie, it's the only sensible thing to do. Unless you want us to have to stay shut up in the bedroom for the next eight hours or so?" He grinned, and she felt the quicksand under her feet begin to give. "Come to think of it, that doesn't sound like such a bad idea."

"All right," she conceded. "But just until morning. So, where did you have in mind? We move into another of the cottages for the duration? I've already shut off the water in all but yours. I waited until last on that one because to open the valves, I have to crawl up under the house, and—"

"Maggie." Smiling with a tenderness that melted the last of her reserve, he hushed her with a finger on her lips. "Just stop making excuses and go pack your stuff. It'll take me about ten minutes, then I'll help you close up things here, we'll set off the bombs and take off, okay?"

She slid out of the Rover before he could come around to help her, feeling far too vulnerable to risk his touch just now. Before they went anywhere together, she was going to have to do some straight thinking, something she found next to impossible when they were together.

"Hey, Maggie!" Halfway up her back steps, she glanced around. Sam was standing where she'd left him, hands on his lean hips, a cold west wind flattening his fatigues against his legs and whipping his hair wildly about his head. "Don't bother to pack a nightgown. It'd be a waste of space."

They argued noisily and cheerfully over where to spend what Sam insisted on calling National Tick and Flea Day. She suggested a hotel in Duck; he countered with one in Chapel Hill. She mentioned a motel in the shadow of the lighthouse on Hatteras, and he told her about the A-frame he owned near Banner Elk. "We could go skiing if you behaved yourself."

They ended up in a brand-new resort not twenty miles from Duncan's Neck, where the Alligator River emptied into the Albemarle Sound.

"This must be the place Deke was telling me about," she murmured, sipping her third glass of Chardonnay. She had stuffed herself with superlative seafood, explored the facilities until her legs were stiff, and now she was perfectly content to sit across from Sam and vegetate. "I'm beginning to see why my property taxes have gone up. The clerk said there's another one going up several miles down on the other side of the river. Not nearly so fancy, but the beach is better."

"Did you notice the name on the sign at the entrance?"

"You mean the Alligator Riviera? I can't believe anyone would go that far, can you? I think I would have gone with something that sounded a little less voracious."

"Actually, I was referring to the second line. The one that mentioned the Wilkerson Group," Sam drawled.

Maggie's lips formed a silent circle. "H. J. Wilkerson, realtor. No wonder my greedy, conniving cousin warned me away from him. Uh—speaking of voracious, are you going to eat that last shrimp?"

"Speaking of voracious, aren't you about ready to go back to the room?" he countered, a lazy gleam in his deep-water eyes.

Maggie was, and they did, strolling slowly past rows of empty rooms. The season wouldn't get under way until spring; nevertheless, they had been welcomed as if they were visiting dignitaries. The new broom syndrome, Maggie had called it. "Or maybe they think we're checking them out for the tourist bureau."

"It's that haughty attitude of yours," Sam had insisted. "They think you're royalty in disguise."

Maggie snorted. "And who do they think you are?"

"Your bodyguard, who else? So get a move on, woman—let me get on with my job."

All during the long winter night, Sam not only guarded her body, he sent it sailing out into the stratosphere time after time with his lovemaking. The paneled room, with its crisp linen draperies, its duck prints and seascapes and modern pine furniture, might have been the richest seraglio for all Maggie knew. Her being began and ended with Sam, with his knowing hands, with his hard body and his marauding mouth.

He undressed her slowly, stroking and kissing each new discovery. There was a small mole on her shoulder just above her right breast that he'd missed before. Now he studied it, tasted it, stroked it lingeringly with his tongue until she shuddered with anticipation. "It's shaped like a fleur-de-lis," he claimed. "The sure sign of royal birth."

"It's shaped like a three-legged turtle, the sure sign of having spent half my formative years in the water."

He examined her foot, kissing the sole until she twisted helplessly. "I thought I detected a bit of webbing just about . . . here." With his tongue, he traced the shape of each small pink toe until she was practically sobbing. Every nerve in her body quivered.

"Help, help," she protested weakly, laughing until tears streamed down her face. "I surrender!"

With a final kiss on her instep, he left her foot and moved up her body, kissing his way north until he was stretched out on top of her. "Thought you might," he purred like a leopard.

They made love again and again, sleeping and waking to lie in each other's arms, talking of nothing and everything. Sam told her something about his childhood, and she talked about the differences between her father's background and her mother's, and how torn she had been trying to fit into two worlds.

She talked again about the baby she had lost, and they held and comforted each other, crying a little for all the lost children. It was an emotional night. There were no barriers.

Neither of them mentioned love.

"Are you happy now, Maggie?" he asked her sometime just before dawn.

"Content," she said after a moment. "I think content is a better term. Happiness is too rich for a steady diet."

"I'll argue that on philosophical grounds," he murmured sleepily. "Remind me when we run out of things to talk about, hmm?"

And then he fell asleep again, and Maggie held him, content for the moment. More than content; happy. When she woke up again, the sun was slicing through an opening between the draperies. She went through the process of sighing, yawning and stretching. And then, seeing Sam sprawled catercorner across the bed on his stomach, naked except for the corner of the sheet that was drawn modestly over one shoulder, she felt herself melt into a smile. Dear Lord, how she adored this man. What an unlikely thing to have happened to her, at this stage of her life.

Careful not to wake him, she sat up in bed, a look of sadness gradually replacing her smile. So what next? Sam hadn't mentioned love. But then, neither had she. Given both their experiences, it was hardly any wonder they shied clear of commitments, and yet Maggie knew she was committed, ready or not. Sam's four weeks would be up on the twentieth of December. What would she do then?

Cope. Deal with it, just as she had dealt with every other crisis in her life. Hurt a lot, cry a lot—and probably curse, too. But she'd eventually heal again. Women did. Only this time it would take much longer. She was older, less resilient. And this time, she'd touched something so rare and wonderful that she knew instinctively it would not come again.

"Breakfast ready, sweetheart?" Sam mumbled, and for one cold instant she was afraid he'd mistaken her for Laurel.

"Sam," she said quietly.

"Hmmm, either call room service, you haughty wench, or come back to bed. Your bodyguard is hungry again."

Maggie was still in the tub when their breakfast was delivered. Sam had delayed her until her water was only lukewarm, and only the sound of the waiter arriving had prevented him from fitting himself into the bathtub with her. As it was, she wasn't sure she'd have the strength to crawl out. For a man of thirty-eight who claimed to have spent most of his adult life in a lab, an office, or on the ski slopes, Sam had turned out to be a most ingenious and creative lover.

It had to end, of course. They checked out after eleven and drove back to Duncan's Neck, taking time to detour through Manteo to visit the dogs.

"I don't think there's any doubt that they recognized us, do you?" Maggie asked as she reached into the back of the Rover for her canvas tote bag.

"That particular breed of dog is noted for its intelligence."

"*What* particular breed?" she jeered.

Sam managed to achieve a look of great injury. "She's obviously a purebred wirehaired Amalgam."

Maggie's eyes sparkled. "And the pups?"

"A more, uh, amalgamated version of their mother?" he suggested, and Maggie laughed until he finally joined her.

The houses were cold but odorless and, theoretically at least, insect-free. While Sam unloaded his gear and opened his own cottage, Maggie collected her spent bombs and tossed them into the garbage can. And then she fished them out again. Knowing Sam, he'd probably accuse her of illegally disposing of hazardous waste.

It was growing dark when he finally joined her. At least a dozen times she'd started to go across to find out what was keeping him. Something had prevented her—the newness, the fragility of what she was feeling, perhaps.

"I miss the little devils already, don't you?" He glanced at the dogs' bed as he stood briskly rubbing his hands together over her stove.

"I know. It's a little scary, isn't it?" She would not mention the nearly two hours that had passed since he'd left her to go air out his house.

"Look, uh—Maggie. I need to go back to Durham. I put through a bunch of calls, but there's no way I can postpone it, so how long will it take you to pack another bag?"

"To what?"

Patiently, he began to repeat what he'd just said, and Maggie interrupted him. "Would you mind telling me what this is all about?"

He *would* mind. That much was obvious from the way he avoided meeting her eyes. "It's only about a five-hour drive. Probably less at night. I've already made you a reservation at the Hilton."

He'd made her a *reservation*? And he *lived* in Durham? "I see. Is it too much to ask why?"

"I'll tell you about it, only not now, okay? Let's just go, and we'll talk on the way."

Anger and yes, fear, drove her tongue. "In other words, trust you. Take off in the middle of the night for God knows how long, much less why—and with a man I've known all of two weeks—"

"Three, dammit!"

She went on as if he hadn't interrupted. "And all because some man I've known *less* than three weeks says, 'come on, Maggie, it's time to jump again.'"

Her refusal had caught him off guard. She could see that he was surprised—maybe even a bit hurt, but dammit, if he was afraid of committing himself, of getting involved, then that was his problem! She was every bit as afraid as he was, and the fact that he was asking her to go home with him and in the same breath, telling her he had booked her into a hotel . . .

Well, that pretty well told her all she needed to know.

Eyes glittering, head held a little too high, she said calmly, "I'm sorry. If you want to go, then that's your business. I certainly won't try to stop you, but neither will I go with you. We've had our fling. Let's be realistic about it, shall we?"

All right, so they were all wrong for each other. It was a little late to be worrying about that now. *Tell me you love me, dammit! Tell me we can make it work!*

He said nothing, but the look he sent her could have cut glass. Without another word, he spun on his heel and walked out. One word, and she would have changed her mind. A single smile would have done it, but he didn't look back. And she didn't go after him.

Ten

——

The time had come, Maggie told herself for the third time in as many hours, to put things into perspective and get on with the rest of her life.

It was not a message she particularly wanted to hear. By the time she had watched her supper grow cold, scraped it out for the Lone Ranger, showered and changed into her gown and robe, she was in no better frame of mind.

Doubts? The pesky things were scattered all over the place. Doubts as to why she had stepped out of her comfortable rut after four years. Doubts as to why she had barged full steam ahead without once asking what would happen afterward.

No—that wasn't quite true. She had asked, all right, only she hadn't bothered to wait for a reply. Smart woman. Really got it all together there, Mary Margaret. No wonder you made VP while others with twice your experience were starting their day with cold calls.

Mother had been right. Living alone could be hazardous to a woman's mental health, and hers had been nothing to brag about even before the advent of Sam in her
life.

"Dammit, I couldn't have been that far off," she muttered angrily, flinging back the quilt to slide between icy
sheets.

In all fairness to herself, she had to admit that Sam was
enough to make a woman lose sight of all reason. For
starters, he was intelligent. That is, if one overlooked a
certain tendency toward pigheadedness. He was un-
doubtedly attractive—if one happened to be drawn to men
with silver corkscrew curls and sardonic expressions. He
was kind to animals, she added dutifully, and he had a
sense of humor and good taste in jazz.

He also didn't have enough common sense to come in
out of the rain. If ever any two people were wrong for
each other, they were. They couldn't go a whole day
without practically coming to blows. She and Carlysle had
hardly ever argued, except near the end, and look what
had happened to them.

Rolling over, Maggie buried her face in the pillow, in-
haling the scent of honeysuckle. She'd used honeysuckle
soap half her adult life, and now, all of a sudden, it reminded her of Sam Canady. Give me a break, she protested silently, remembering which one of them had been
responsible for their winding up in bed together. Responsible! She'd been all over him like rust on a barbwire
fence! Not that he'd put up too much of a fight.

National Flea and Tick Day. And oh, what a celebra-
tion! Like a fool, she had thought she could play about in
the shallows and not be in any danger of drowning. Some
people never learned. Now Sam was gone, and he probably wasn't coming back, and she didn't know how she

was going to get through the next few days. Or weeks. Or years.

One thing she did know—she was never going to get to sleep at this rate. Her real problem was starvation. She hadn't eaten anything since the middle of the morning, when Sam had fed her bites of country-cured ham dripping with honey, and in return, she'd laughingly peeled him half a dozen grapes.

Barefoot and bundled into her heavy bathrobe, she worked her way, stalk by stalk, through a bunch of celery, grinding her teeth as if it were Sam's neck between her molars. The least he could have done was to tell her right out that he was leaving because things were getting too sticky. He probably knew how she felt about him and was running for his life, she thought, taking perverse pleasure in her own unreasonableness.

"Pack a bag. Do this, do that," she muttered around a mouthful of celery. "Don't ask questions, woman, hop to it. Move! Chop chop."

Although she had to admit that he had invited her to go with him. Tipping the last of the stalk, she nibbled the end.

Invited? He'd *ordered* her to go, knowing very well how she'd react to being told what to do. It was called eating your cake and having it, too. He'd asked, knowing she would refuse.

Exhausted from arguing a lost cause, Maggie got up, dumped the celery leaves into her soup pot and foraged again, this time coming up with a jar of hot pickles that had been in the back of the refrigerator for at least a year. The lid had rusted tight. Unable to budge it, even with her rubber gloves, she felt an irrational urge to weep.

"Damn all curly-haired environmental consultants named Sam Canady," she muttered. Leaving the pickle

jar unopened, she poured milk into a small pan and set it
on the stove to heat. Then, on impulse, she added a dollop of bourbon, a dash of cloves and a lump of sugar. One
way or another she was going to sleep tonight!

Waiting for her bedtime drink to heat, she began making a mental list of things to do tomorrow. Number one,
check on the dogs. Number two, forget Sam Canady.
Number three, get back to work on that darned chicken-
headed sea gull and see if she could turn it into an osprey.

Sam got all the way to Williamston before reaching the
end of his tether. Swerving into the first lighted service
station he came to, he searched frantically for a pay
phone, finally spotting the familiar glass bubble beside the
air compressor. A sleepy-sounding operator found a list-
ing for M. M. Duncan, and he misdialed twice before he
got through. By the time he did, he was having second
thoughts. What the devil could he say to her after he said
he was sorry? He knew what he wanted to say, all right—
and should have said a hundred times before now.

Only he'd never spoken those words to a woman before. Well…maybe to his mother, when he was about six
or so. This was different. Somehow, he didn't think he
was going to be able to say it from a pay telephone in an
all-night service station with a curious attendant looking
on while he pretended to coil the air hose.

Wind cut through the open weave of his sweater.
Christmas decorations swung wildly from the street-
lights, looking even more forlorn than he was feeling at
the moment.

Maggie, Maggie, dammit, answer your phone! He'd
had no business leaving her there all alone, not with some
creep sneaking around slashing tires and making threatening phone calls. This whole thing with Maggie had hit

him so hard he didn't know which end was up, and then he'd got the call from his secretary's niece, and one thing had led to another. He'd snapped, Maggie had snapped back, and like a jackass, he'd got his back up and stalked off, leaving her all alone and defenseless. Dammit, he ought to be dragged out at dawn and shot!

"H'lo, whosis?"

"Maggie? Maggie, listen to me—"

"Who *is* this?"

"Who the devil did you expect? No, I didn't mean that. Look, Maggie, don't hang up, okay? Whatever you do, just don't hang up on me."

"Sam, are you all right?"

She was awake now. He could almost see her eyes widen, see the way she'd lift her chin—wary, ready to fend off the whole world. God, he wanted her in his arms right now. If he could only touch her—if he felt her warmth, her strength, he would know what to say. "Maggie, I'm sorry I blew up the way I did."

"Did you?"

Not *are* you, but *did* you. He smiled a bit grimly. She wasn't going to give an inch. He couldn't honestly blame her. "Yeah, for what it's worth, I did. And I am. My only excuse is that I was worried and I had a lot on my mind, and I thought you'd understand."

"I understand perfectly."

God, this was impossible! He shifted his weight to his other foot, turned his back to the street and waited until an empty logger rumbled past. "No, honey, I don't think you do. Look, if I came back to the Neck—I'm in Williamston right now, but I can be there in an hour. Maggie, we need to talk."

Some seventy-odd miles away, Maggie leaned against the refrigerator, her bare toes curled against the cold linoleum, and forced herself not to give in. "Sam, I don't know why you left, or why you bothered to call and wake me up in the middle of the night, or what you want from me, but getting a speeding ticket or breaking your neck isn't going to solve anything. Why don't you just do what you have to do and then if you feel like getting in touch, I'll probably be here."

Sam felt the kind of tightness in his gut that Rolaids weren't going to help. While he'd never had all that many relationships with women he'd never considered himself backward in that respect. Until now. "Darlin', listen to me. Out of a staff of seven men and four women, I've got exactly three people working for me right now, and one of those is a high-school girl majoring in boys and bubble gum. The rest are laid up with flu. I've got an industrial waste situation that needs to be dealt with before a lot more people wind up in the hospital with something a lot worse than flu. All the field and lab data are in, analyses done, the recommendations written up, and the final report was already in the works. And then my whole damned crew gets wiped out and everything grinds to a halt."

"So that was your emergency," Maggie said after a long pause. "You could have told me, Sam. I'd have understood."

"I know, sweetheart. There's more—hell, I may as well tell you. Laurel's stuff is just the way she—just where it's been for the past few years. I've been trying to get hold of the maid to have her pack it up and get rid of it, but I guess she's laid up, too."

He could hear her breathing on the other end. Or maybe that was his nerves ticking over. "Look, I made a mess of things. Nerves, more than likely. I'm not real good with people—maybe you noticed."

At that she laughed softly, and he could feel relief flowing over him like warm rain. "There might be room for improvement."

Sam could have jumped up and down and shouted. The report was a cinch. With a good temp, he'd have it out in two days. As for the other, he'd find someone to handle it before he took Maggie home with him. It was time. It was past time.

He made a deliberate effort to relax, steeling himself to say the words he'd been holding back, words he'd been saying in his head for days now. But before he could speak, Maggie's voice came over the line. At her words, spoken softly, he sagged against the glass bubble. "Sam, go do whatever you have to do. When—if you want to come back, I'll be waiting."

His hands were sweating! "Maggie—sweetheart, you don't know how much that means to me," he said with fierce relief. "I want you with me. I hate like hell leaving you there by yourself, but I don't want you exposed to whatever bug has laid half of Durham low."

"What about you?"

"I'll take vitamins. I'll wear a raincoat. I'll do whatever it takes to wind this thing up by the end of the week and get back to you. Maggie, I . . ." He glanced over his shoulder at the station attendant, who was now polishing the air compressor with a greasy cloth. "Maggie, I—" To hell with the man. Let him listen. "Maggie, I love you," he all but shouted before slamming down the phone.

While the attendant topped up his gas tank, Sam mopped the sweat off his forehead. It was a clear, crisp twenty-nine degrees outside, and he had more than a hundred miles to drive. He suddenly felt as if he could easily have flown the entire distance.

* * *

After so many hours of smiling, Maggie's cheeks were tired. Even her teeth were dry. She put aside the chicken-gull-hawk and poured herself a glass of milk. Obviously she wasn't going to be able to focus her mind today. She might as well do drudge work, something that didn't require concentration.

Back in November she'd bought a roll of plastic to cover the windows. Since she wasn't sure she trusted herself on a ladder in her slightly dippy condition, she decided to start with the two windows that opened onto the front porch. If she managed to accomplish that much without botching it, she might tackle something a bit more demanding.

He loved her.

Had he actually said that, or had she only dreamed it? No—she couldn't have dreamed it. Bourbon-laced bedtime drink notwithstanding, she hadn't been able to go back to sleep at all after Sam had called. Now, pausing in her search for the heavy-duty staple gun, she leaned her elbows on the sawdusty workbench and gazed dreamily at the neat row of tools.

Sam loved her. And Sam Canady wasn't the type of man who would say something like that just for effect. In many ways, she hardly knew him at all, yet in the deepest sense, she had known him from the first time she'd ever seen him. It was as if she had recognized him subconsciously. If she were of a dreamy, mystical bent instead of being painfully practical, she'd be tempted to call it fate.

Not that it was all clear sailing from here on out. There were problems—maybe too many problems. His work, for one thing. She couldn't see him moving his consulting offices to Duncan's Neck, nor could she see herself blindly selling out to Deke and following a man she had known only a few weeks to a place she had never even seen, to do who-knows-what with the rest of her life.

Besides, they really didn't get along very well. Except in bed. She wasn't good wife material—she'd already proved that much.

But then, Sam hadn't mentioned marriage.

Still—what if he did? What if she said yes, and then failed again? There was such a thing as caring *too* much. Sometimes the harder one tried to succeed, the more apt one was to fail, and if she failed this time...

One step at a time, she cautioned herself. First the storm windows. Then, if she managed that much, she might tackle a serious relationship.

With a languid movement totally unlike her usual brisk efficiency, Maggie reached for the staple gun, gathered the roll of plastic under her arm, and wandered out onto the front porch, forgetting to put on her coat. Fortunately the slanting rays of the winter sun kept her from freezing before she came to her senses.

Not until she had dropped the roll to the floor and begun unrolling it with one toe did she notice the trail of red drops across the porch.

Red paint. The same shade that had been used on her door. Disbelievingly, Maggie lifted her eyes to her freshly painted marine blue door.

And then she wished she hadn't. "Oh, for crying out loud," she wailed, dropping scissors and staple gun with a clatter. All the radiance went out of her morning. She felt like crying. She felt like knocking heads together, wringing necks, cursing a blue streak and *then* crying!

She spotted the discarded paint can out in the yard and collected it, touching it gingerly in case there were any fingerprints. Turning back to the house, she stared at the

ugly words, feeling as if she had been physically as-
saulted.

This Hose Is Cundimed.

"The department of education is condemned!" Anger
rose up afresh and she strode back inside to dial the
emergency number she had pasted on the base of the
phone. It was busy, of course. She redialed and got another busy signal. After four tries, she slammed the phone
into its plastic cradle and marched into the bedroom for
her purse. This time the sheriff would darned well see the
handwriting on the wall for himself, if she had to hand-
cuff him and drag him out here bodily! One way or another, Maggie was going to have satisfaction, because
enough was enough.

With Christmas only a few weeks off, the streets of
Manteo were crowded. A mob had gathered on the side-
walk outside the courthouse, and not until Maggie had
parked her car and walked half a block did she notice that
they all wore uniforms. All except the one in the middle,
who looked awfully familiar. Suddenly everything fell into
place and she felt like a fool for not having seen it before.
She'd even *defended* the varmint!

Recognizing her target, she waded into the milling
crowd that consisted of National Park Service personnel,
game wardens and several of Dare County's finest,
planting herself in front of the culprit. "Pogie, I hope
they hang you by your damned beard until you turn
blue!"

The lanky, long-haired old man in the filthy denims
eyed her warily. "Now, Miz Maggie—"

"How *dare* you do such a thing! Even when I knew
you'd been around, I couldn't believe you would ever
stoop so low as to do something—"

"Now, calm down, Miz Maggie. I ain't got nary a thing against you personal-like."

"Pogie," she said with deadly intent, shouldering aside a deputy who had stepped forward to bar her way.

"Miz Maggie, why don't you just go home and we kin talk about it terrectly," the old trapper pleaded. The indescribable smell of him reached out to her and she took a step backward.

"Miz Duncan, if you know anything about this business, I'd appreciate taking a minute of your time?"

"*Know* anything!" Maggie turned to glare at the deputy who had addressed her. "That—that stinking old illiterate has done it again!"

"Now you ain't got no call to insult a man, Miz Maggie. My folks wuz churched good 'n' proper."

"You found another one?" That from one of the game wardens.

"Right in the same place! And I had just repainted it after the first time, too. This is going to cost somebody, if I have to take it out of his rotten hide." She jerked her head to indicate which somebody it was going to cost.

"Now wait a minute. Hold on there. You say this bear actually came into your house?"

"Onto my porch. And I think polecat is a more apt description."

"Is he still there? Ma'am, you should've called and let us send out a team. You've lived around here long enough to know better than to go messing around with bears, especially if they'ze been injured."

"Wait a minute, have I missed something?" Maggie protested, now thoroughly confused. "I thought we were talking about Pogie. He's practically confessed. What's more, I saw him leaving the Neck yesterday afternoon, and he was in an awfully big hurry. Once I walked around to the front porch this morning, it was easy to see why. There were only two sets of tracks on the road to the Neck when I checked. My new retreads and the bald tires on Pogie's old truck.''

By now, Maggie had the attention of every man and woman there. ''And if it's evidence you need,'' she told her audience with growing satisfaction, ''then I suggest you check his hands. I have a feeling you'll find red paint on them, because the can was leaking, and that old goat wouldn't wash if his life depended on it! He didn't even bother to hide the can, either. Litterer!'' This last was directed at the old trapper, who looked guilty of every crime in the book and a few that hadn't yet been recorded.

It was Sheriff Austin himself who wedged his way through the crowd and took her aside. ''Okay now, Maggie, let me get this straight. You think Pogie's your vandal?''

''Well, don't you?'' Perplexed, she stared at him. ''Why else did you bring him in? Not for poaching—he's been getting away with that for years.''

''Not that I want it spread around, but he's also been a valuable source of information, Maggie. He's a natural. He's always being hauled in for one thing or another—people get used to seeing him around here. Besides, what he's got away with isn't as much as most people think. In season or out, he's a lousy trapper and a worse hunter. No animal's going to come within range of any man who smells like a distillery.''

''Information about what?''

''It hasn't been made public yet,'' the harried officer said quietly, ''but we've been cooperating with several other agencies in a crackdown on bear poaching.''

"*Bear* poaching!" At his pained look, Maggie lowered her voice. "Why on earth would anyone go to the trouble? They don't even have antlers."

"No, but they have gallbladders, which happen to be in great demand in certain parts of the world. A man can clear as much as five, six hundred dollars apiece for the hide and gallbladder of a fully grown black. Another year or so and they'd be in the same shape as the red wolves a few years back."

Maggie's shoulders sagged. Alongside wiping out the black-bear population, a little paint on her front door seemed rather trivial. "So that was what Pogie was doing when I thought he was painting obscene slogans on my front door. So much for my skills as a detective."

"Now that this bear thing's all wrapped up, maybe I can spare a man to look into it. As for Pogie, I can't see the old bas—uh, buzzard doing something like that. Where's the profit? Pogie never does anything that won't buy him a couple of bottles of Blue Thunder. And why on earth would anyone pay Pogie to bother you?" He grinned, his bushy eyebrows arching even higher. "So what is it this time? Spelling improved any?"

"Not noticeably," Maggie admitted with a reluctant answering smile. "Whoever he is, I'm still not sure if he's referring to my hose or my house, but whichever, this time I think it's condemned. I'll leave the spelling up to your imagination."

They were interrupted by an attractive young woman wearing a Smokey the Bear hat. She stuck her head in the door and said, "By the way—our informant does have red paint on his hands, if it means anything to either of you."

* * *

An hour later Maggie was finishing a chocolate milk shake in Hardee's. Deke sat across the table from her, looking more than a little shaken, for once.

"I still can't believe it. I knew Wilkerson was interested in buying up anything along the river with development potential, but it never occurred to me that A.B. would try to make a deal with him. Everyone in the office knew I was taking Millie and the kids to Acapulco next month. A.B. also knew that the options I took out on the other cottages were running out. Evidently he'd planned on renewing them in his own name and then making a deal with Wilkerson as soon as he could scare you into selling—hopefully before I got back."

"I still don't see why he couldn't buy up all those willing to sell and leave the rest of us alone."

"You were the only holdout," Deke said a bit sheepishly. "I had a buyer on the hook, but unless I could get a clear title to the whole Neck, my buyer wasn't interested."

"You mean the church?" Maggie inquired with wicked innocence.

Deke studied his flawlessly manicured fingernails. "All right, so maybe I tried to pressure you a tiny bit. Mary Margaret, you've got to know I'd never do anything to hurt you. If I'd even suspected—" He fumbled with his collar, leaving his expensive silk tie slightly askew. "Well, it's over now. A.B.'s out. I told him to clear out his desk before I got back to the office."

Maggie sighed. "He seemed so nice. A bit dense, maybe—and sort of stingy when it came to supplying firewood to the renters, but pleasant enough."

"Yes, well . . . like I said, it's over. If you want to hang on to the old relic, you've got my blessing. We're still friends—that's what's important."

As indeed it was.

Sam called that night, and she told him about catching her vandal red-handed, so to speak. He told her about Didi, his secretary's niece, who had managed single-handedly to overturn a four-drawer filing cabinet—spilling its contents across the floor, to shred a valuable report—step on his wristwatch and louse up his automatic dialer. And that was only the first day.

"It's probably her first job. She's nervous."

"*She's* nervous! I don't even walk under light fixtures when she's around."

Maggie laughed, and Sam managed a small chuckle, eventually. "Sam, don't let anyone breathe on you," she cautioned. She wanted to urge him to hurry up and finish whatever it was he had to do and get back to her, but she didn't dare. It was all too new.

"Don't forget to check on Princess and the babies."

"They're home again, Henry included. I've got an appointment for the next shots, and after that they're in the clear."

"Maggie, I—"

Her fingernails turned white as she gripped the phone. Say it! Say it so that maybe I can begin to believe in us, she pleaded silently.

"Maggie, I think I might be able to get away by Friday. About suppertime?"

"Fine. I'll see if I can get some fish to cook." Her voice was perfectly calm, but her palms were drenched with sweat.

Jubal had taught her as a child to cherish every moment, for once past, it could never be recalled. Now she found herself wishing she could spin the hands on her clock and make it Friday. She cleaned the house and raked the yard, trimming the dead leaves off the backhouse lilies, as well. On Thursday she went into Manteo and bought yards of satin ribbon, tying perfect bows around each puppy's neck. The ribbons lasted all of five minutes. Princess was sporting a brand-new collar, which she was doing her best to scratch off. At least she was beginning to smell more like her cedar bedding and less like kennel deodorant.

On Friday she washed her hair, gave it a lemon rinse and dried it in the sun. She soaked in bubble bath and shaved her legs. When she was lotioned and moisturized, she frowned in the mirror at the fine lines forming around her eyes. She was going to have to start wearing her sunglasses more.

Instead of seafood, she decided to show off with her one and only chicken-and-rice recipe. Sam had never even seen the urban side of Maggie Duncan.

The wine was chilling and the chicken simmering in its broth when she finally heard the Rover pull up beside the truck. Her heart went into overdrive, and she took several slow, deep breaths. One step at a time, she cautioned herself. She would remain cool, but gracious. They would have a pleasant dinner and then talk things over in a calm, objective manner.

Peering through the window, Maggie watched him slide one long leg out the front seat and then twist around to retrieve his bag from the back. Calm? Unfortunately, just the sight of that lean, fit torso was enough to make her knees turn to rubber.

He was grinning as he leaped up onto the back porch, and she made herself turn away from the window and pretend an intense interest in the chicken tarragon simmering in its wine sauce.

Calm, she reminded herself. Don't rush your fences.

Her hands were actually trembling when she opened the door. For one long moment they could only stare at each other, and then she was in his arms.

"I kept thinking, she'll be gone—she's not real, she's something I dreamed up in my mind—the perfect woman," Sam said in a low, rough voice, his face buried in her hair.

"Oh, Sam, if you only knew...I've been calling myself all kinds of a fool for daring to dream. I've been examining all my flaws and—and telling myself I had my chance and blew it, and—"

"I might have been exposed to the flu, and now I'm exposing you, but I couldn't stay away. God, I love you, Maggie!" He crushed her against him, his hands moving over her back, her shoulders, her hips, as if assuring himself that she was all right, all there—just as he remembered.

"Sam, I love you," she blurted out. "I know none of this makes sense, and I promised myself I wouldn't get emotional about it, but—"

"Go ahead, darlin', get emotional. Let me help you." He kissed her then, and it was a long and hungry kiss, a making-up-for-lost-time kiss. A promise-of-things-to-come kiss.

"You probably just gave me the flu," she said when she could speak again.

"In that case, we'll just have to get plenty of bed rest."

Sam held her so tightly she could hardly breathe, then held her away and beamed down at her. "God, I love tall, cranky, emotional women."

"Cranky? Are you talking about me?" She could drown in his eyes and never even realize it. "You're the cranky one. That was the first thing I noticed about you."

"We've got a lot in common, haven't we?" His hands were moving up and down her sides with exquisite slowness, his fingertips barely brushing her breasts on the upward sweep.

"We have absolutely nothing in common," she retorted.

"We both like that stuff you call coffee. Name me one other man in the world who can make that statement."

"I'm used to living by myself. I like being alone," she countered.

"Me, too. Natural born loner. We can be alone together—it's more fun that way."

"You're incredibly argumentative," Maggie accused, but she was laughing, and so was Sam. "If this keeps up, I'll have to use my dish towel on you."

"I've got a better idea," Sam confided. "Why don't we skip the crime and get on with the punishment. You mentioned a padded cell with bars at both ends?"

He led her, still clothed and laughing helplessly, into the bedroom, where they flopped across the billowing mattress. "It's great to be home, Maggie."

"Which brings up another subject."

"One thing at a time, hmm?" He was working on her buttons, his fingers clumsy in their haste.

Maggie couldn't argue with that. Hadn't she been cautioning herself all along to take one step at a time?

"I couldn't sleep for remembering," Sam whispered when he finally managed to remove the last shred of clothing between them. He gazed down at the subtle curves, the ivory, the coral, the amber. "I can't believe I've found you, after all these years of carrying your image in my heart."

Maggie felt a response kindling in her, one that had nothing to do with the length of time they had known each other, their different pasts, the experiences that had brought them to this point in their lives. So they would argue. At least they would never be bored with each other. She didn't know how she knew that, but suddenly she was quite sure.

"Do you know something strange," she confided a long time later. They had made love with a wild intensity that had left them both in shock for a while. And then Sam had begun to caress her all over again, and the second time was even more beautiful in its own way.

"Tell me something strange," he murmured now.

"You made me mad as the devil that first day, when I met you on the beach. You were the most disagreeable man I'd ever met, and I was utterly fascinated by you. Does that make sense?"

"Makes great sense to me. I thought you were a meter reader, and then the wife of a fishing guide with half a dozen children stashed away somewhere. I also thought you had the sweetest rear end and the loveliest legs and the foulest disposition of any witch I'd ever met."

"In other words, it was a classic case of love at first sight," she said with a low chuckle. As her face was buried against his throat at the time, Sam's reaction was all she could have wished for and more.

"Woman, if you want to start something, you're going to have to feed me first. Is that burned chicken I smell?"

Maggie bolted from the bed, stark naked, and ran into the kitchen to rescue the ashes of her fine dinner. "Sam—get the mop!"

"Did it explode?" He had taken time to wrap a sheet around his body before following her.

"Sweetpea did—there by the table leg. As for the chicken, I doubt if even the Lone Ranger will touch it now."

"How about bacon and eggs for two?"

From her bed in the corner, Princess lifted her head and whimpered hopefully. "How about bacon and eggs for three?" Maggie countered. By then the rest of the pups had come piling out of the box again and were pulling at Sam's toga.

"How come a couple of cranky loners ended up with a full house?" Sam grumbled as he applied the mop.

Watching her cranky loner try to mop with one hand and preserve his modesty with the other, Maggie laughed. "You love it. You're just too grouchy to admit it."

His mouth turned down at the corners, but his eyes told her all she needed to know. "So do you, my long-legged termagant."

For once they were in perfect agreement.

Epilogue

Grab Marian when she scoots past you. I don't want her out in the boat without a coat of sunscreen." Maggie stroked a final dab of the stuff on Jubal's nose and let him escape. At three and a half years old, motion was the twins' natural state of being.

"Life preservers, lemonade, sunscreen—are you sure we're ready for this fishing expedition? Have you notified the Coast Guard to halt all intracoastal traffic until we're safely back on shore?"

"Is that a snide remark, Canady?" Maggie teased.

"Snide? Whatever gives you that idea—Canady?" Sam retorted, his eyes dancing with warmth and humor as he gazed at his tall, tanned wife. Pregnancy agreed with her, even at this stage. "Honey, are you sure it's all right for you to be going out with us? We'll be okay out there if you'd rather stay here and take a nap."

"Afraid of being skunked again?"

"Whaddya mean, *again*?" Sam shot back, easily corralling a whirlwind with black curly hair as she tried to dash out the screened door. He took the tube of sunscreen and began applying it to his loudly protesting daughter while Maggie located her scarf and stuffed it into her canvas bag. "The one I almost caught yesterday weighed a good five pounds. You saw what he did to my tackle before he got away."

"Oh, you mean the crab pot you snagged?"

Sam released the squirming child and grabbed his wife, lowering his face so that their noses were touching. "Crab pot, huh? There's only one crab pot around here, and we both knew where that is." He stroked her round belly.

Laughing softly, Maggie rubbed her protuberance against his spare middle. "Did you ever guess that first day when you attacked me with an armload of driftwood that we'd end up owning the whole Neck?"

"Ever regret it?"

Maggie gazed over his shoulder through the screened porch to the six shingled cottages, each one different, that were nestled attractively in their newly landscaped surroundings. "Not a minute of it. I like Durham—I love being able to teach a class in investments when I want to and carve when I want to.... I love being involved with the nature museum and the children's activities. But this place has a special meaning to me."

"To me, too, sweetheart," Sam said deeply. "It's where I found the one thing I'd been searching for all my life." His kiss was no less ardent for the fact that physical closeness was becoming increasingly difficult in this last month of pregnancy.

"A sparring partner?" she teased.

"We do have some beauts, don't we?"

They did. They argued cheerfully over a multitude of small issues, secure in the knowledge that the soul-deep unity that had drawn them together would hold and be stronger for it.

Sam shaped her face between his large, capable hands. His expression was tender, his voice gruff with emotion. "Have I told you lately how much I—"

"Hey, you two," called out MacGuffie Duncan. "If you're going fishing with us, get a move on. Granny says she can't sit on those two much longer without some help."

Laughing, Sam and Maggie left the coolness of the renovated old house for the brilliance of a late-May morning. "For a couple of cranky loners, we did all right, didn't we, love?" she said softly.

Sam's fingers tightened on her hand in silent agreement.

* * * * *

Keepsake

FOUR UNIQUE SERIES
FOR EVERY WOMAN YOU ARE . . .

Silhouette Romance

Love, at its most tender, provocative, emotional . . . in stories that will make you laugh and cry while bringing you the magic of falling in love.

6 titles per month

Silhouette Special Edition

Sophisticated, substantial and packed with emotion, these powerful novels of life and love will capture your imagination and steal your heart.

6 titles per month

Silhouette Desire

Open the door to romance and passion. Humorous, emotional, compelling—yet always a believable and sensuous story—Silhouette Desire never fails to deliver on the promise of love.

6 titles per month

Silhouette Intimate Moments

Enter a world of excitement, of romance heightened by suspense, adventure and the passions every woman dreams of. Let us sweep you away.

4 titles per month

ATTRACTIVE, SPACE SAVING BOOK RACK

Display your most prized novels on this handsome and sturdy book rack. The hand-rubbed walnut finish will blend into your library decor with quiet elegance, providing a practical organizer for your favorite hard-or soft-covered books.

Only $9.95

Approximately 16" x 8" when assembled

Assembles in seconds!

To order, rush your name, address and zip code, along with a check or money order for $10.70* ($9.95 plus 75¢ postage and handling) payable to *Silhouette Books.*

Silhouette Books
Book Rack Offer
901 Fuhrmann Blvd.
P.O. Box 1396
Buffalo, NY 14269-1396

Offer not available in Canada.

*New York and Iowa residents add appropriate sales tax.

BKR-2A

Silhouette Desire®

1989
IS THE YEAR
OF THE MAN!

What makes a romance? A special man, of course, and Silhouette Desire celebrates that fact with *twelve* of them! From Mr. January to Mr. December, every month spotlights the Silhouette Desire hero—our **MAN OF THE MONTH.**

Sexy, macho, charming, irritating…irresistible! Nothing can stop these men from sweeping you away. Created by some of your favorite authors, each man is custom-made for pleasure—*reading* pleasure—so don't miss a single one.

Diana Palmer kicks off the new year, and you can look forward to magnificent men from **Joan Hohl, Jennifer Greene** and many, many more. So get out there and find your man!

Silhouette Desire's
MAN OF THE MONTH…